C000099144

THE
SAILING DAYS
OF
BIANCA DRAKE

by Louise McGee

The Sailing Days Of Bianca Drake © 2021 Louise McGee

All rights reserved. This book or any portion thereof may not be reproduced or used in any manner whatsoever without the express written permission of the publisher except for the use of brief quotations in a book review.

ISBN (Print): 978-1-09835-796-2
ISBN (eBook): 978-1-09835-797-9

CHAPTER ONE
Welcome Aboard!

DATE:8 JANUARY 1998
EMBARKATION DAY
PORT OF CALL: SOUTHAMPTON
ALL ABOARD TIME: 3.45PM

There I was, freezing in the icy January winds that swept up the harbour, staring up at what was to be my new home for the next six months. I wasn't looking up at a fancy apartment, a cute little condo, or even a nice new house. I was looking up at a fifty thousand tonne, two-thousand-passenger cruise ship, the kind that takes senior citizens and posh people on holiday to all sorts of exotic locations around the world.

I felt rather insignificant gazing up at this gigantic boat. It was SO much bigger than I'd imagined. This was where I would be living, eating, and sleeping from now on. I'd spend all of my days and nights on this huge piece of tin floating around the world's oceans. How crazy was that? My stomach hit the floor from the enormity of it all, but it was too late now. There was no turning back. My work contract was set in stone and I was about to embark on the biggest adventure of my life.

I had always wanted to travel, but here I was, twenty three, and hadn't been anywhere more exciting than Bournemouth on a wet weekend. There was the time when I applied to be an air hostess, but a panic attack, brought by the sudden realisation that I was terrified of flying, somewhat overshadowed my interview. And there was the time when I was all set to go backpacking, but chickened out last minute when I couldn't fit all my cosmetics in the rucksack. Seriously, how do girls sacrifice all those essentials? Hats off to them, I couldn't do it.

My grandmother had warned me I couldn't possibly do a backpacking trip, as there wasn't a rucksack on earth big enough to fit all my clothes in. And she was right. In fact, it was my nana who came up with the secretary job on a cruise ship idea. The next best option, she said. "You can travel the world with unlimited baggage allowance." GENIUS!

After a lot of paperwork, classroom study, passing medicals and applying for visas, I had to learn how to do all sorts of near impossible stuff: jumping off high-dive boards in steel toe cap boots (which combined two of my biggest fears – heights and deep water) and single-handedly inflating life rafts and rescuing "dead" bodies out of the water. Hardest of all perhaps were the months of waiting.

But then, at last, little Bianca Drake was about to embark upon the great ship Lady Anne to sail the Seven Seas for, wait for it.........

New York, Columbia, Mexico, San Francisco, Hawaii, Fiji, New Zealand, Australia, Malaysia, India, and the list went on. I was about to experience places a young girl like me from Liverpool could only usually dream about!

"It's time for us to say goodbye, Bianca. They're asking all visitors to leave the gate." My mother and nana hugged me as tightly as they could. "Be good and be brave. Ring as soon as you can to let us know how it is."

I couldn't say anything back due to the huge lump in my throat, so I just nodded, holding my mother's hand tightly, not wanting to let go. The gates opened for the crew to embark the ship and my nerves were shot to pieces. The tannoy repeated the announcement for all visitors to exit the ship yard. My Mum had to turn and walk away, leaving me standing there all alone.

I found my voice. "I'll be fine, Mum. I'll call you as soon as I can," I shouted, holding back my tears as she turned and waved. I was determined not to cry. I didn't want to make them any more upset. She was already having a nervous breakdown at her only daughter flying the nest, so I didn't want to make it any worse for her by blubbering like a baby.

That was to be the last time I would see an old familiar face for months. I felt absolutely terrified, yet beyond excited all at the same time. I'd never lived away from home before. And had certainly never sailed on any sort of sea.

The most boating I'd ever done prior to this was a school kayaking trip in deepest, darkest Wales - which didn't end well. And my geographical skills left a lot to be desired, a fact I only came to realise during my cruise ship training. Up until then, I was certain that the Falkland Islands were right next to the Isle of Man. Who knew?

The gates closed and it was just me, myself, and I. I dragged my bags over to join a line of tired looking men and women who I assumed were the other crew members; they didn't seem very excited to be there. I flashed my biggest smile to my fellow shipmates, accompanied with an awkward hello. This didn't quite get the response I was hoping for; some of them stared at me blankly whilst most of them just looked through me as if I was invisible.

"Why are they all looking so miserable? What the hell have I let myself in for?" I asked myself, muttering under my breath.

"We're not all like that, girl."

I jumped as a voice piped up from behind me and turned around to come face to face with a very pretty red-headed girl about my age.

"I'm sorry... I was just... well, I was smiling and nobody acknowledged me." I stumbled for an excuse, holding my hand out. She was so glamorous! I felt scruffy in comparison. But I took a deep breath and said confidently, "I'm Bianca. I'm new."

"I can tell you're new by all them bags." She laughed. "You'll never fit all that stuff in your cabin, girl. We live in rabbit hutches. Didn't anybody warn you?" I was struggling to understand what she was saying, as she had the thickest Irish accent I'd ever heard.

"I'm Madison by the way, or you can call me Maddie. I'm one of the beauty therapists in the spa." Phew, at least that explained why she looked so perfect. She had just one small suitcase with her. I'd definitely gotten carried away with the packing.

"This is my fourth contract, all on the same ship mind, so I know the place inside out." She was looking me up and down. I really wished I had paid more attention to my embarkation outfit or at least got my hair done before I got on board.

"Where are you going to be working?" Maddie asked.

"I'm going to be the cruise director's secretary." I got the job description out of my bag to read over it.

"Jeez. That's a job and a half." She looked taken aback. "How did you get that gig? You must only be my age?" This girl was impressed, but I was perplexed by her comment. What exactly had I let myself in for?

"I'm used to working a lot and long days." I hoped I sounded more confident than I felt.

She smiled reassuringly. "I'm sure you'll be grand once you get settled into it." Maddie took one of my cases and gestured for me to follow. "They're calling for us to join. Stick with me and I'll show you the way,"

Thank goodness I'd met this girl. I wouldn't have had a clue where I was going. We went through a series of security checks to have our bags scanned, eventually arriving at the entrance to the ship where we were greeted by an important-looking man in a white uniform and peaked cap who checked off our names.

"What do we do now?" I whispered to Maddie.

"We wait and then he'll let us cross the gangway when it's safe to do so," she explained.

The gangway was just a rickety piece of wood that joined the land to the great big ship. It didn't look the safest. I could just see that piece of wood caving in with the weight of my bags. And the safety net strategically placed underneath did little to inspire me with confidence.

"Goodbye, dry land. Till we meet again," I whispered to the dockside, eyes tightly closed so as not to look down at the ten-metre drop beneath me. After a tense couple of minutes, I made it. Finally, I was on board Lady Anne.

I lurched over and grabbed the nearest handrail, holding on for dear life with my eyes squeezed shut again. This was about to be my first proper experience on the water and I couldn't lose my balance this early.

"What are you doing?" Maddie asked, looking worried.

"I'm getting my sea legs," I replied.

"Oh I see," said Maddie, laughing. "Well, you might be better doing that at 5.00pm when we actually leave; we're still tied up to the dock for eight hours."

I opened my eyes and sheepishly let go of the rail. I laughed too, hoping she didn't think I was too much of a nutcase.

Maddie directed me to the room where all the new joiners were to assemble. I was relieved to find that I wasn't the only new kid on the block. There were at least ten others, every one of them looking as lost as me. I took a seat.

"If you need me, I'm up on the spa deck. Good luck, Bianca, girl." Maddie patted me on the arm and off she trotted.

Fifteen minutes passed and I began to think I'd been forgotten about. One by one, all the other newbies had been collected, yet I was still sitting there all alone in an empty room. I was just about to give up and try to find Maddie, when a tall blonde guy dressed in a smart navy suit started walking towards me with a clipboard.

"Miss Drake?" He held out his hand.

"Yes, that's me." I shook his hand perhaps too enthusiastically.

"I'm Pete, the Assistant Cruise Director. I'm sorry for the delay. We had a problem with missing luggage. How are you feeling? First time on a ship?" he asked.

"I'm a bit nervous actually," I admitted. "Yes, it's my first time on a ship."

"Do you suffer from sea sickness?" Pete picked his pen up and started scribbling down notes.

"To be honest, I've never spent enough time on a boat to find out. I was ok on the ferry over to Dublin once, but that was years ago." As those words came out of my mouth, I realised how pathetic I sounded. I probably should have considered that small factor before I decided to take on a job at sea.

"Well, only time will tell," Pete smiled. "Cynthia, our Cruise Director and head of department, isn't available to meet you today but as her second in charge, I'll take you to your cabin then to the safety drill. Then we'll pop to the office to go through all the paperwork." Pete took my cases off me and led me out of the room. It sounded like it was going to be a very busy day.

"Bianca, have you packed for two years?" Pete asked, trying not to appear out of breath as he pulled my bags along. We passed through a maze of corridors all packed with crew members zipping in different directions, clunking through lots of heavy doors. Eventually we got to a tiny passageway on the right with three cabin doors.

"The cabin on the end is yours; you're sharing with one of the receptionists from the front office."

My face dropped. "I was assured in my interview I'd have a single room and that I wouldn't have to share with anybody!" I exclaimed.

"I'm sorry, not at the moment. You're next on the list for a single cabin when one becomes available, but for now you're sharing." Pete looked very serious. "This has twin beds and a port hole with actual daylight coming in. This is very unusual for a crew cabin. I suggest you enjoy it while you can." He opened the door and ushered me in.

I got to the door and was surprised to see I wasn't alone. There was a girl sitting at the dressing table. She jumped up, rather startled by my entrance.

"I'm sorry. I should've knocked." I hesitated in the doorway.

"Don't be silly, mate, it's your room, too. I'm Lisa, nice to meet you," Lisa had brown wavy hair with an amazing tan; she definitely had a surfer vibe going on. "I'm from Sydney, Australia. How about you?"

"I'm Bianca, pleased to meet you." We shook hands firmly. "I'm from England."

I'd never left my country before, never mind met anyone from Australia, yet there I was sharing a room with someone from the other side of the world.

"I'm going to catch you later, mate," Lisa said in her fantastic Aussie drawl. "I'm just going to grab a bite to eat." She left me alone in the cabin.

I sat on my bed trying to accustom myself to my new surroundings. At least I hoped it was my bed and not Lisa's. I peered out of the port hole, the tiny glass circle just above sea level that would give me a view of wherever we were travelling to in the world. How amazing was that?

I quickly got changed into my new uniform: white blouse with a navy blue skirt and matching jacket. I pinned on my name badge that read 'Bianca Drake - Secretary'. I looked at myself in the mirror, put on a touch of my favourite red lipstick, and took a deep breath. Looking back at my reflection, I felt very lucky to be on board this beautiful, majestic ship.

BLEEP, BLEEP, BLEEEEEEEPPPPPPPPPPPPPP.

I almost jumped out my skin. What the hell was that?

"A very good afternoon, ladies and gentlemen. This is Captain Cooper speaking. I'm delighted to welcome you all on board our magnificent vessel, Lady Anne. In twenty minutes time we will be exercising the ship's company in our safety procedures. When the ship whistle sounds, please take your lifejacket and head towards your designated muster station."

I panicked and started ransacking the room for my safety gear. Just as I was groping under the bunk bed with my bum sticking up in the air, Pete appeared at the door with an orange life jacket and a luminous yellow hat.

"These are for you, Bianca. Follow me and I'll show you exactly what to do." He put the cap on my head. "First of all, as soon as you hear that alarm going off you should put on your lifejacket as if this is a real life emergency."

Pete passed me the jacket as though I knew what to do with it. I struggled at first, but with a bit of thought I got it on. I looked at Pete, feeling rather chuffed with myself.

"Bianca, that jacket is on back to front and the waist strap is around your neck like a noose."

This wasn't going to go down well at all.

I followed Pete down several corridors until we got to a foyer which led us into a huge restaurant. It was split into two levels with a massive marble staircase in the middle. It was so luxurious, all purple velvet with mahogany carvings - I didn't feel at all posh enough to be in there.

The venue was full of other crew in hi-vis life jackets and caps. Even more faces I didn't recognise - and they were all staring over. Pete got out a microphone and began to give instructions to the crew over the PA system. When he'd finished, he came over to talk to me again.

"Any minute now, the whistle will sound and the restaurant will fill up with our passengers," Pete informed me. "Just watch and learn. Everything I do now, you will be doing next week, including my microphone address, so please pay attention."

Me, instructing a safety drill? I didn't know one end of the ship from another. It seemed I had a lot to learn and fast. That god awful noise rang through my ears again as the captain repeated his speech over the tannoy.

No sooner had the captain's talk finished than the restaurant began to fill up with passengers. Hundreds of them. The majority were elderly people, many of whom had walking aids. Wheelchairs and walking frames were parked at every door as dear little old ladies and men shuffled in on their sticks or on a supportive arm to find somewhere to sit.

Once all the guests were seated, the captain gave his safety announcement, then Pete reeled out a speech about mustering, lifeboats and stepping off the ship in an emergency. Oh dear, I really hadn't thought about that part of the job, either.

"Ladies and gentlemen, please observe the crew members as they now demonstrate the wearing of the lifejacket."

Pete stared towards me, signalling for me to remove my life-jacket. I quickly pulled it off, immediately regretting it and wondering how the hell I was going to get it back on again. I was supposed to be showing passengers the correct way to put on a lifejacket, but I didn't feel comfortable doing it considering that on my first attempt, only a few minutes earlier, I'd almost choked myself to death.

"Place the lifejacket over your head, then connect the velcro strips together." By now, Pete was glaring at me.

"Pass the belt around your waist and close it at the buckle," Pete continued.

I wasn't prepared for this or quite sure what was going on, so I copied the crew member opposite me, but somehow I ended up with the strap wrapped around my neck again.

"There is a light on your lifejacket," Pete told the guests.

Was there? I couldn't find it. I think that was because I had the lifejacket on upside down. All the other crew members were pointing at this light on their perfectly assembled jackets, yet I was still fumbling around trying to work out what I'd done to myself, becoming more flustered, embarrassed, and tangled up a treat.

"There is also a whistle for attracting attention on the pocket on the side," Pete continued. By now he seemed to be purposely avoiding looking over in my direction, despite my obvious struggling. He was desperately trying to keep a straight face.

I found the whistle! YES! Now this I could demonstrate, no sweat.

PEEEEEEEEPPPPPPPPPP

I blew the whistle as loud as I could. The old ladies at the next table jumped out of their seats in shock. I felt the whole room staring at me. I hoped I hadn't burst anyone's hearing aids. I'd certainly succeeded in attracting attention. I got that bit right. On second thought, maybe I wasn't supposed to do that.

"Ladies and gentlemen, please do not be alarmed. Bianca is just testing the safety equipment on her jacket," Pete assured the audience whilst giving me daggers across the room.

I was definitely not supposed to do that. I think I was just supposed to point to it, but it was too late, so I smiled and waved at everyone, when all I really wanted was for the ground to swallow me up.

"Oops," I said sheepishly to the sea of faces looking at me.

It was the guests' turn to put on their lifejackets with the crew's assistance. But I was still in such a mess that two elderly gentlemen, both sporting handlebar moustaches and nautical blazers, were helping me out of mine instead of me helping them into theirs!

"Don't worry, love, we've all been there on our first day at sea," chuckled one of the men.

"How the heck did you get that waist belt in a knot around your neck?" said the other chap. "That's a double half-hitch constrictor knot if I ever saw one."

I couldn't answer as the strap was pulling tighter on my windpipe and I was becoming desperate for breath. The men were making it even worse. Just as I could feel myself blacking out, Pete spotted the situation and came to unravel me.

"She put on a good show, didn't she, sir?" Pete joked with the guests as he deftly undid the front and finally freed me.

"I'm so sorry," I spluttered to Pete, gasping for much needed air.

As the guests filtered out the restaurant, Pete turned to me and smiled.

"Bianca Drake, that was possibly the funniest lifejacket demonstration I've ever seen in all my years at sea. Can you do that again next cruise?"

CHAPTER TWO
First Impressions

DATE: 8 JANUARY 1998
EMBARKATION DAY
PORT OF CALL: SOUTHAMPTON
ALL ABOARD: 3.45PM

"As I'm sure you're aware, Bianca, you've joined the ship at a very exciting time, as we're about to embark on our annual world voyage," Pete explained as we made our way from the safety drill to the office. "Firstly, we'll have a short stop at Hamburg, then we depart for our 107 night circumnavigation of the globe. You must be very excited. Have you done much travelling?"

"No, sir, I've never left home before." I sounded like such a novice as those words came out of my mouth.

"Then you've a lot to learn, my dear. I hope you don't get too homesick." Pete opened the door to the office, pointing to my new desk opposite the door.

"I won't get homesick; I've been waiting for this for such a long time." I sat down in my chair realising that the thought of missing home hadn't yet occurred to me. I was going to be far too busy with my new job.

"We've a small office, as you can see. Three of us work from here. Myself, you, and our cruise host, Max. We usually have a translator, Vinnie, for our international guests, but he's on sick leave."

The desks were packed closely together, and without any windows, it was quite dark inside. My workspace was spotless, meticulously organised with colour-coded drawers and files. I was mesmerised by the huge map of the world, pinpointing all of our ports of call.

"First things first, read these." Pete passed me several text books:

Safety at Sea

Life on Board

Daily Job Expectations

After reading those (incredibly long) books, I felt like I'd mistakenly signed up for the Merchant Navy, not a fun job on a cruise ship. There were so many rules and regulations and so many safety procedures to remember, I really didn't know how I was going to take in all the information.

The office door swung open, and in strutted a guy about my age dressed very sharply in a black tailored suit; very Mediterranean-looking, olive-skinned with slicked back hair and the whitest teeth I'd ever seen.

"You must be Bianca." He put his hand out, leaning over my desk towards me. "I'm Max, dance host with the most, jack of all trades, yet master of none. I'm very pleased to meet you."

"Hello, Max. Nice to meet you, too. I look forward to working with you." I smiled and shook his hand.

"I can show you around when Pete is busy." He pulled up his desk chair and sat next to me. "I've been working on board the Lady for a couple of years now, so there's not a lot I don't know about the old dear - feel free to ask away." Max looked through the text books I'd been reading earlier. "Don't be too alarmed by all these guidelines. It'll all come together after a couple of weeks, so please don't worry. It can be very daunting being new."

I warmed to Max as it became clear he was trying to make me feel at ease. He was so stylish, he looked more suited to working on a fashion magazine than a cruise ship - I got the feeling that I definitely wasn't his type.

Pete reminded me it was time to go and meet my new boss in her office next door. Cynthia La Plante. She sounded very important. I gently tapped on the door.

"Come in, Miss Drake!" a voice shouted.

I crept in, feeling like the new girl on the first day at school. Cynthia was standing behind a huge oak desk with her arms folded. She was nothing like I'd pictured in my head. She was a very tall and slender elderly lady with long dark hair down her back. She appeared to be dressed in a pair of orange flowery curtains from my nana's living room circa 1975.

She had quite pointy features with striking blue eyes. I could tell she must've been very attractive in her younger days. She shot me a look over her glasses, inspecting me from head to toe.

"Hello, Cynthia, I'm Bianca. Pleased to meet you." I put out my hand to greet her, to no reaction.

She sat down and gestured for me to do the same. I waited quietly whilst she examined my CV that was laid out on her desk.

"Welcome on board, Miss Drake." She finally broke the awkward silence. "I assume you've been shown and are now familiar with all your safety duties which are first and foremost our priority."

I nodded eagerly, praying she didn't know about the choking incident at the drill.

"You've a lot of expertise in the hospitality field, then?" Cynthia questioned in a very loud, raspy voice - she seemed to be shouting at me even though I was only two feet away from her.

If expertise meant I did part time reception at a hotel last summer then sure I was, so I nodded again, wondering what I'd gotten myself into. Her face was very stern; the complete opposite of the reassuring smile I was hoping for.

"You've been selected from many hopeful applicants to fill this position on board the magnificent cruise liner Lady Anne. Not only is this ship the finest at sea, it's also the flagship, no less. The most refined and prestigious cruise line sailing the seven seas. Kings, queens, lords, and ladies have sailed on our beautiful vessels for centuries. Our clientele are very refined and sophisticated." She positioned her glare right at me.

"And I'm fortunate enough to hold the position of cruise director on board this wonderful vessel, a position which I take incredibly seriously. Myself and my department are the faces of Lady Anne. We're the life and soul of the cruise and the passengers' enjoyment, therefore it's imperative that we're helpful, respectful, and courteous at all times, whether on duty or not."

I was looking straight back into Cynthia's eyes, still nodding, my heart pounding with nerves.

"Let's get a few things straight about your job." She cleared her throat.

"Your role is to play the vital cog between many different wheels, the missing piece of the jigsaw, so to speak. You need to know not only the ship, but the workings of each and every department inside and out."

I gulped - no pressure there then. I thought I'd applied for the secretary job, yet Cynthia was making me sound like the bloody captain.

"Do you have any idea of how many of these departments you'll need to converse with on a day-to-day basis?" she asked as I quickly shook my head.

"You'll be dealing with the bridge team, the security department, the purser's office, the tour office, the engineers office, the housekeeping department, the shop team, the spa team, the bar team, the restaurant managers, our executive chef team, the photography team, the casino team, the art department, and the list goes on."

I sat there wide-eyed. How the hell did they even fit that many staff on board? Never mind the fact that I had to work with all of them every day.

"There is no room for error in this role. You're my secretary and personal assistant, therefore you've an incredibly big job to do." She seemed to be waiting for me to flinch or buckle out of the door.

"I'm fully aware of this, Cynthia, and I'm ready to take the bull by the horns," I replied, forcing myself to keep a straight face.

"Good, glad to hear it! Miss Drake, as I said earlier, you've joined a very busy department on a very prestigious ship. You'll be on parade at all times, immaculate in your appearance and of course always willing to help both guests and crew alike."

I was still doing my nodding dog impression. I couldn't have got a word in edgeways if I'd tried. I wondered if I'd bitten off more than I could chew...

I remained calm and collected, I wasn't going to let Cynthia's words get to me. I was on board Lady Anne and ready to give it my best shot. I was far too excited to let my new boss frighten me off.

"We're all artistes, Miss Drake. Each and every one of us in this department come from very creative and show business backgrounds," she continued. "You'll be surrounded on a day to day basis by musicians, singers, actors, dancers. You're at centre stage in a hub of creative activity."

She referred to the several framed photographs of herself dotted around the office and mounted on the wall. Photographs of her on stage, acting, singing, and dancing. I spotted a photo of her swinging upside down from a trapeze - she must've been a circus performer back in the day. Looking around her office, it seemed to be some kind of shrine to herself, which I found slightly creepy.

"The bar is exceptionally high and I expect you to continue this standard." I was beginning to feel slightly out of place from Cynthia's comments, as I had no 'showbiz' background apart from my turn as Cinderella in the school play when I was fourteen.

She handed me a ship's pager that enabled direct contact with me at any time. I was instructed to never switch this off or I'd be in serious trouble.

"Welcome aboard, Miss Drake, and remember the show must go on!" Her voice echoed down the corridor as I left the office.

I stood outside holding the door behind me for a minute, slightly bewildered. I hoped my new boss wasn't as tough as she seemed, yet that first meeting didn't give me much faith. I decided to carry on regardless and give Cynthia the benefit of the doubt. Besides, I was just too excited as I was about to start my travels of the big wide world all on my own.

No sooner had I returned to my desk and plonked myself at my the computer than the phone rang. It was my new boss.

"Bianca, it slipped my mind to mention that you're also the weather reporter on the daily TV show for the guests. You're to introduce yourself and give our guests a quick weather report. Max will fill you in and show you where the film crew shoot. Filming starts in ten minutes on Deck Ten Aft."

The call disconnected before I even had a chance to say anything. TV Show? Weather reporter? Me? IN TEN MINUTES!

"I've to do a weather report I knew nothing about," I wailed at Max, who was busy tapping away at his computer.

"Let's go. I'll take you." He dropped what he was doing, grabbed my arm, and off we went.

I floated up to the filming room, dazed and confused, trying not to show Max how nervous I was. I was racking my brains trying to work out how I missed weather reporting on my job description. I definitely didn't put meteorologist on my CV. I hated public speaking and now I was going on TV for a couple of thousand guests. To say I was nervous would be putting it mildly. I was shaking like a leaf in the elevator.

"All you do is introduce yourself. Tell them what your job is on board, where you're from, that kind of thing. Just be yourself. Be natural," Max advised. "Cynthia landed this on me on my first day. After a few attempts this'll be a piece of cake, I promise." Max was so reassuring. "Oh and whatever you do, don't swear!"

"But how do I know what the weather's going to be like?" I panicked.

"I'll ring the navigator on the bridge and get you the weather. Don't worry."

The filming room was just like a mini TV studio. There were lights, cameras, and even studio backdrops. Max explained that each morning the passengers tuned in and watched Cynthia describe all of the daily activities and information on the port and such. I was to give the passengers a quick run-down of the weather each day in port so they knew what to wear or if they needed an umbrella.

I was so nervous my tongue was stuck to the roof of my mouth and my knees were knocking; it was not a good look, I can tell you. The cameraman started wiring me up. He placed a battery pack round my waist, clipped a small microphone to my shirt collar, then put me next to the huge weather map board. I caught a glimpse of myself on screen. I was horrified. I hadn't even had time to do my make-up!

I began panicking and going completely blank, then I went light headed and felt like I was going to faint. I couldn't focus properly as I had this bright spotlight shining in my face.

"3 – 2 – 1 Action!" The cameraman signalled over to me to begin. I smiled manically but there was no use in me trying to speak because my tongue was still plastered to the top of my mouth. Good job it wasn't live or I would've looked like a mad woman. I tried to talk but nothing would come out. The knee knocking wasn't helping.

"I think I need some water!" I gasped.

Eleven takes and thirty minutes later, I finally nailed it and even got the weather right. Thank God for Max and his impromptu cue cards. I was so grateful that he was there to help me with the whole debacle. I liked him more and more by the minute. I was sure we would become great friends.

After my presenting ordeal I just wanted to lie down in a dark room, but when I got back to the office there was a huge pile of letters waiting for me that had to be hand delivered to each cabin on the ship.

Pete looked at me sheepishly. "You're the mail girl this evening, but don't worry, Max will help you deliver."

"Oh great," I replied, trying to sound as enthusiastic as I could. "Wow, the decks actually go up all the way to twelve? I'll get lost," I noticed as I examined the addresses on the envelopes.

"So you met Cynthia earlier then? How was it?" Pete asked as I began organising the mail.

"It was ok, I suppose. I think she liked me," I replied sarcastically.

Two hours later we finally delivered the last letter. We'd walked the length of the ship fifteen times over, reached every level from deck one all the way up to twelve. I couldn't feel my feet and I was absolutely exhausted.

"Right, we deserve a drink," Max said. "I'm going to take you to the infamous bar of crew. I want to introduce you to one of my good friends on board. She's going to meet us there."

"Where?" I asked.

"The crew bar of course. Where all the cool kids hang out."

I'd no idea what he was talking about. I was told repeatedly in my ship training that the crew are too busy for a social life. Never mind drinking in a bar.

Max led me down a corridor which led to a huge heavy fire door that required two of us to prize it open.

"This is my shortcut. Don't tell anyone."

We crept through the fire door, down another corridor, then to a green door which ejected us into a room heaving with people everywhere. We had to push our way in to get anywhere near the bar.

The bar itself was dark and dingy with a pool table, darts corner, DJ box; in fact, it was just like a pub back home. People stood around chatting and drinking, most of them still dressed in their work uniforms. There was a small stage next to the bar with music blaring out of a huge speaker.

"Is it always like this? Why is it so busy?" I shouted above the noise.

"There are a thousand crew on board this ship, Bianca, and this is where they come to relax."

I could hear so many different languages around me, Russian, Polish, Spanish, all laughing, joking and clinking beers. After we got served with our drinks, Max managed to grab the last free seats in the far corner.

"Why's everyone staring over?" I asked Max, starting to feel as though I was in a fishbowl.

"Why do you think? You're the new girl on the ship." Max laughed. "You, my friend, are a breath of fresh air to the usual scenery."

"Oh really? Not interested, thanks." I snorted in disgust.

"We'll see in a few weeks when you spy a cute one." Max grinned.

At the very moment Max said that, I spotted a guy in the middle of the crowd. Dark haired, tall and handsome, a typical model type. I could feel myself going very red faced just looking at him. It was a good job he didn't see me; this guy was seriously gorgeous.

I wondered if he was English or if he was talking to his friends in a different language? I told myself to snap out of it, I wasn't there to get mixed up with any boys. I was there to do a job and visit all these amazing places we were en route to. Guys were the last thing on my mind, but my word, he was so good-looking.

"Oh - that boy! He's fairly new." Max spotted me staring over. "Very handsome. He's probably got two girlfriends, Bianca, and that's just on the ship. You've got a lot to learn about the goings on at sea."

"I'm not here to meet a guy anyway, Max. I had enough of all the deadbeats back home." I laughed it off.

"Here she is. My friend I want you to meet." Max stood up and began waving to a girl at the bar. As she made her way closer to the table, I was happy to see it was the lovely Irish girl I'd met earlier on the gangway.

"This is Madison," Max introduced us.

"Ah the new girl! You ok? We met this morning." Maddie shook my hand anyway. "How's your first day been, girl?"

"It's been a bit full on. Thanks again for your help," I admitted. "Max is just educating me about the crew bar."

"All the crew gather in the same little groups, standing in the exact same place every night," Max explained to me. "Over by the darts board are the bar waiters, next to them are the housekeepers, the chefs sit in the far corner over there, the shop staff sit round the bar and the spa girls by the juke box. It's pretty much the same every night, you'll see."

"Where are all the officers in the white uniforms?" I asked, envisioning all the sailors in the white rig out you see in the movies.

"They usually come later on; they work unsociable hours." Maddie rolled her eyes. "You want to stay away from that lot, girl. They're with everyone."

My eyes wandered back to the gorgeous guy at the bar.

"Don't get Maddie started on ship relationships. She's had bit of a nightmare lately." Max laughed.

"Here, I'll tell you, girl," Maddie cut in. "See that guy and his girl at the end of the bar?" She pointed over to a very loved-up looking couple with their arms draped round one another and gazing into each other's eyes.

"Love's young dream, right?" She tutted. "That's his wife, married for two years. They met on board."

I thought that was a lovely story, having your other half with you whilst experiencing all these wonderful places.

"See that girl scowling over the other end of the bar?" Max smirked, referring to a tall blonde girl at the bar with her arms folded and looking very upset.

"That's his girlfriend. When the wife goes home for her vacation, that's his other woman," Maddie said, very matter of fact.

"What? Does his wife know?" I was quite shocked.

"No, but girlfriend number two does and so does everyone else on the ship," Max added. "She waits for the wife to disembark, then makes her move. The husband has his own cabin, you see. Double bed, window, and access to room service."

"So, let me get this straight. What you're saying is that the other woman doesn't mind he's married as long as she gets a bigger bed and room service?" I asked.

Max and Maddie both nodded. They proceeded to educate me about the trials and tribulations of people working at sea or as they called it 'ship life'. I sat there open-mouthed, listening in disbelief. Although life at sea was long working hours, the social life was let's say busy, with dating dilemmas, love triangles, affairs, people leading double lives; it was the stuff of good stories.

We finished our drinks and got up to leave with most of the bar watching. By total accident I caught the gorgeous guy's eye; immediately my heart began to race and I was going redder by the second. I was so flustered I walked straight into the door and smacked my nose really, really hard. I heard sniggers coming from the crowd behind me, but I was too ashamed to look back and rushed out the door.

"He definitely gave you a look then, Bianca, just before you smashed your face in," Maddie spluttered in between fits of laughter.

"I feel ashamed," I cried in pain, yet half in hysterics, bent over outside the bar. We trailed back to our cabins through a very complicated maze of doors and staircases. Thank goodness I had my two new friends as a guide to get me back to my room safely.

We said our goodnight and I crept into the cabin being extra quiet so I wouldn't wake Lisa, which didn't actually matter because Lisa was on her bed looking very cosy with a guy who was serenading her on a ukulele. They did the decent thing and left as soon as I arrived.

How awkward it was sharing a room with a girl I'd never met before. I got changed then climbed into bed and started thinking about the next day; my first ever port of call.

CHAPTER THREE
Happy Hamburg!

DATE:9 JANUARY 1998

PORT OF CALL:HAMBURG,GERMANY

ARRIVAL:8.00AM

DEPARTURE:OVERNIGHT STAY (9.00AM THE FOLLOWING MORNING)

At 6.30am I was literally shaken out of my bed. I hit the floor half asleep with a big thud. The whole cabin was shaking, rattling, and shuddering around me. It felt like I was in the middle of a hurricane. Apparently, it was just the engine thrusters pulling into the ship's dock.

I thought a thruster was the dance move that my Uncle John did at weddings, yet they were also an integral part of docking a cruise ship. Lisa told me we'd be woken in this same manner every time Lady Anne was docking in a port. I was going to need helmets and shin pads for bed.

My first day of work and I didn't know what to expect. I was feeling slightly paranoid about having to get ready in the same room as Lisa. Although she'd been really welcoming and friendly, it was still rather awkward.

The television was still catching the news channel on the satellite, so I sat at the dressing table to put my make up on while I had a nice cup of tea. Suddenly the show broke over to some breaking news;

'The famous cruise ship Lady Anne has run aground early this morning. The cause of the problem may have been due to strong winds that were prevalent around the coast line. Tug boats have been attached to the ship in an effort to put it back on course.'

A cruise ship story on my first morning at sea. I was laughing to myself about the coincidence whilst I put on my mascara.

"What was the name of that ship?" Lisa shouted from the bathroom.

"Lady Anne, I think. Wait, isn't that us?" I screamed, dropping my make up all over the carpet as I realised it was.

We dived to the porthole to get a better look. Sure enough, there were tiny tug boats pulling us away from the coastline. That was our ship we were on! Journalists were reporting on national news and we never felt a thing, totally oblivious that our little ship was causing breaking news.

"Ladies and gentlemen, please do not be alarmed. The tugboats are assisting us in this minor incident and we shall be back on our course and underway very shortly," Captain Cooper announced over the PA.

"I hoped my mum didn't see that! She'll be worried sick I've been shipwrecked on my first morning at sea," I shouted to Lisa.

I arrived at the office to begin my day of work. Cynthia was pacing up and down the corridor outside looking rather annoyed.

"I've been paging you. Why did you ignore me?" she asked sternly.

"I didn't ignore you Cynthia, honestly. I didn't hear the beeper," I protested.

"Well, keep your ears out in the future. Lucy, the sports host, has pulled a muscle in her back and can't do the aerobics class that's scheduled in the ballroom this morning."

"Would you like me to remove the sign from outside the class?" I offered.

"Certainly not. I want you to put your name on the sign instead. I can't cancel the class. You're covering Lucy's class and it starts in twenty minutes."

"Me?" I asked, shell-shocked.

"Your resume clearly states in black and white that you're an aerobics fanatic."

Oh dear. I thought it was such a good idea to include in the interests section the two weeks when I did keep-fit down my local gym (but never went back again).

My exaggerations were slowly coming back to bite me in the backside. I doubted anyone would believe I was a keen clay pigeon shooter, yet that was there in black and white, too.

"Nobody else is free." Her voice trailed off as she waited for me to surrender.

"I'll go and get ready," I squeaked.

I raced back to my room and threw on shorts and a vest. I jotted down a minimal effort routine that I could run through, bearing in mind the average age of my class would be around eighty three.

As I was scrambling around for some socks, I came across a pair of pink wristbands of Lisa's, so I borrowed them to make me look a bit more convincing. I did a quick practise in the mirror, trying to memorise all my mother's 80's keep fit videos, but it wasn't working. I was all over the place.

Once I had a routine of sorts nailed in my head, I was a bit more confident I could get away with this aerobics instructor facade. I headed to the ballroom, going over and over the workout I'd put together in minutes.

"Good morning, ladies and gentlemen, and a very warm welcome to this morning's aerobics class!" My voice boomed down the headset, putting my weather presenting skills to the test.

"Lucy can't make it today, but I'll be swapping out my weather reports this morning to help you guys keep fit," I shouted in my chirpiest fitness guru voice. Everyone was clapping and cheering. They all seemed so pleased it was the weather girl teaching the class. "Let's get started with a warm up."

I talked the class through the warm up with some very basic moves. I was so unfit I could barely touch my toes. The stretches seemed to go well and everyone appeared to be enjoying the class. So far, so good. As the music began to speed up, so did the routine.

"It's time to reach up to the sky and back down and touch your toes," I instructed, hearing little moans and gripes from the crowd.

"Come on now, we're just getting started," I cheered enthusiastically, trying to get the crowd going. We did a few more easy steps, then I decided to really get them going and introduce my mother's favourite exercise move of all time.

"Now, we're really going to get the blood flowing. Let's go into a star jump." I was jumping all over the stage with my arms and legs flapping everywhere, hoping Cynthia was watching from afar to see how well I was doing. I was so busy peering up to the balconies, that I hadn't noticed that half the class had stopped and were crowding around one spot.

"Can we just stop it there for five minutes?" I stopped abruptly to see what had happened. I was horrified to find an elderly lady lying on the floor crying out in pain. I called for a nearby bar waiter to call the medical centre.

"Are you ok, madame? What happened?" I asked as I bent over to see what the problem was.

"I can't move my hip. I think it popped out when I was star jumping," the lady wailed. "I've just had a hip operation. I thought it'd set back into place."

I couldn't believe it. It was all going so well and now this poor lady was about to become hip-less and it was all my fault. Cynthia was going to murder me.

I attempted to console the injured party and make her as comfortable as possible until the medical team arrived. When they did, they manoeuvred her into a stretcher to have her examined by the doctor. I felt so guilty and also terrified about what Cynthia was going to do when she found out.

"Can we continue on? We were having a great time," one of the keep fit ladies asked.

"I'm sorry, that's it for today. I'll need to check on the patient." I was worried sick. I packed the room away quickly and headed back to my cabin to keep a low profile, hoping to stay out of Cynthia's way for as long as possible. What a mess, and it was only 11.00am.

Max came knocking on my cabin as I was changing out of my fitness gear.

"Bianca, tell me it's not true. Tell me you didn't dislocate dear old Gloria's hip with your acrobatic moves?" He giggled. "Nice sweat bands by the way."

"It's not funny, Max. It really wasn't like that." I pulled the bands off my wrists. "Dislocated? At least it hasn't totally fell out then." I flaked out on the bed. "That's a relief, I suppose. Cynthia's going to have me for this."

"Fear not, as I bring good news." Max looked rather proud of himself. "Cynthia did have smoke coming out of her ears, but guess what? She shouldn't ever have sent you; you're not a certified instructor. If anything, Cynthia's the one in trouble with the doctor, so you my dear are in the clear. Hamburg harbour for drinks tonight then? It looks like you need a stiff drink already." And off he went.

I lay flat on my bed for a few minutes, staring at the ceiling, reassuring myself that it was only my first day at sea and it'd all settle down very soon. I wasn't sure if I could take much more and I hadn't hit the first port yet.

After a long afternoon in the office, learning the ropes with Pete and filing reports, I was almost ready to go out into Germany for the evening. I hadn't actually seen Cynthia since the morning, just the very long to do list that was left on my desk with strict instructions to go on a ship tour the following morning. I was so excited I'd get to meet Captain Cooper in person.

"I'm going to get ready for tonight now, Bianca." Pete packed up his desk. "Listen, about Gloria. She's going to be fine. After your day it's only right I should show you round on your first port of call." We arranged to meet on deck two, midships. I agreed, wondering how to locate deck two on my own.

I ran up to the filming studio room to do my second weather recording. I was still just as knock-kneed, hoping I'd come across like I knew what I was doing.

"Don't forget, ladies and gentlemen, to wrap up warm if you're going ashore this evening. We're expecting light snow showers around 10.00pm this evening. Have a happy Hamburg," I signed off and removed the microphone pack. I was becoming quite the pro, and it was only day two.

I wrapped up well in my winter gear and went to find the meeting place. Pete was already there waiting, his arm linked with a very tall and slim brunette. I wished I had known he was bringing a supermodel. I would have worn stilettos.

"Bianca, this is Nadia." Pete introduced us. "She is part of our dance team."

Nadia smiled and bent down to air kiss me, as she was about six foot tall.

"She doesn't speak much English, but she's so beautiful," Pete whispered to me whilst Nadia wasn't listening.

"Sorry I'm late." Max hurried towards us. "Maddie can't make it. She's to give a lecture on colonic irrigation."

"What?" I asked. "Is she an expert?"

"No, but she's a spa therapist and they pretty much can turn their hand to anything."

Off we went into the port of Hamburg with Pete and his dancer striding ahead of myself and Max. The streets were so pretty, lined with snow against dozens of little wooden huts. The markets were jam packed with tourists drinking beers from the biggest pint glasses I'd ever seen and queuing at the German sausage stalls. The strong smell of cinnamon wafted up my nostrils.

"We're heading to our usual Hamburg haunt," Max explained. "Hamburg is one of the best nights out ever. Let's promise each other that no matter what happens, we'll get back on board by 2.00am."

"I can't be out till that late. I'm meeting the captain tomorrow. I've got to make a good impression." We shook hands to seal our curfew promise.

We got to Hamburg Town Hall just as the sun was going down, then headed for our first drink. The huts were so inviting inside, complete with a huge log fire burning in the middle.

Pete ordered a round of mulled wine.

"It gives me great pleasure to introduce Bianca to Hamburg." We clunked our mugs together and drank. "Down the hatch."

I chugged whilst everyone else sipped. My nerves were gone. It was my first night out in a foreign country. Thankfully, the mug of hot red hit me like a smack across the face and I began to relax a bit.

"Anyone fancy another?" I headed back the bar for round two.

After the second wine and a chat in broken English/Russian with Nadia, it was time to move on to our next stop. On the way out the door an elderly man dressed in a Sherlock Holmes get up grabbed me by the arm.

"Aren't you that girl from the safety drill?" he asked. "You were so funny with that lifejacket. Was that an act?"

"Bianca's such a comedian. She does that little routine every week," Pete said to the guests.

"Can I have a picture with you? I've got a granddaughter just like you." I had my photograph taken with the man and his friends.

"Bianca, when you're quite finished with your fans, it's time for the Reaperbahn." Pete hailed a taxi as we got outside.

"A barn?" I asked, thinking we were on our way to a hoedown.

"Not a barn dance, Bianca. The Reaperbahn is Hamburg's red light district." Pete laughed.

"What are we going there for?" I questioned. "Are you going to hire me out for the night?"

"You wish." Pete laughed. "You're such a newbie, relax."

We hopped into a taxi. By now Nadia was chatting away to me. I think the alcohol had improved her communication skills as she was talking lots of English: which made me wonder, if I drank enough, would it make me fluent in Russian? There was only one way to find out...

The snow had started lightly as we got out of the taxi with music blaring from every venue. There were so many pubs, clubs, and bars to choose from, with plenty of semi-naked, PVC-clad women outside, coaxing people in. The taxi driver very nicely warned us not to head up to the area on the left, as it was strictly forbidden to tourists. We took his stern advice and headed in the opposite direction.

"I don't think I could face another wine." My cheeks were still burning bright from the last round.

"That's ok, we're moving onto the heavy stuff now." Pete pointed to a bar across the street with a neon sign flashing above the door saying 'The Rat Pit'.

"We're about to enter a Rat Pit in a red light district," I muttered to myself. "I hope I get out alive."

"Of course you will." Max squeezed my hand. "We're going to have a great night."

The male population of the bar (which was all of them except the bar lady), looked very interested in us as we walked in. All of them stared at the gazelle-like Nadia following in behind me. I knew I should've worn my heels.

"One, two, three – Happy Hamburg," the barmaid shouted as we clinked our shot glasses and knocked back some black liqueur.

"Welcome to the Rat Pit," the barmaid said. "Where've you come from?"

"We're crew from the ship. We were here last year, actually." Max winked at the bar lady as she giggled.

"Of course, I remember now." She smiled. "The drinks are on the house."

Now, I did have the best intentions of going home early, but that was quickly going out of the window. I mean, it would've been incredibly rude not to stay out when the night was just getting going. Right?

"This is where it gets interesting," Max whispered as the lights were dimmed and heavy metal blared out from every speaker.

"Are you ready to go downstairs?" the barmaid asked Max.

She signalled for us to follow her behind the bar, and shuffled us into a room out the back. She pulled open a huge velvet curtain, which unveiled a horizontal door with a big brass handle.

"We're not going in there, are we?" I was slightly panicked. I'd seen many a horror film with this setup.

"Welcome to the Gates Of Eden," the barmaid said. "The most hush hush club in the whole of Hamburg."

"We come here every time," Max said. "This place is something else."

We followed the barmaid down a stone spiral staircase to find a bouncer guy in a hood at the bottom. He pulled out some very strange looking masks with different animal faces.

"What are these for?" I whispered to Pete.

"You can't reveal your identity in here," Pete whispered in my ear. "Remove it at your own risk."

It all sounded very dodgy to me, yet I reluctantly put the mask on. The masks were eagles, snakes, lizards, each one with a different totem pole style face. Once the masks were on, the doors opened and then the night began.

The club was booming, blue and green strobe lights flashed. There was a green grass lawn for a dance floor, decorated with lots of exotic plants and trees. The party goers were an array of weird and wonderful characters. The attire of choice seemed to be leather chaps and lots of feather boas. I spotted a few rubber gimp suit wearers complete with zips. This place was mental and I loved it.

Max and I downed the free champagne which was being served by topless waiters wearing rubber rabbit masks. Fire eaters were serving shots, then doing backflips.

I hit the dance floor, busting moves out very similar to my exercise class earlier. It was so hot in there, I had sweat pouring off me, so I tried to find a bathroom to cool down.

In the queue for the restrooms, I ended up chatting to a very nice German girl. She told me all about the time she came to England as an exchange student. She also had an electric fan which she very nicely kept letting me use to cool off.

As my turn came for the toilet, she asked if I'd mind sharing, so she squeezed herself into the cubicle with me. Big mistake. As I tried to exit, she blocked my door and leaned in for a kiss.

"What are you doing?" I was so taken aback.

"Don't tell me you didn't feel it, too?" She looked surprised. "The connection between us. It's electric."

"No, that was your fan that was electric!" I dodged her advances. Despite my reaction, she went in again. This time I ducked under her arm and made it out of the bathroom in a panic.

I hurried ahead, not looking back, ending up in a totally different dance room than before. She marched after me, looking rather pissed off, so I was ducking and diving between the clubbers, trying to lose her as quickly as possible. I finally made it back to the original dance floor, looking for Max.

"Why won't you come with me?" She jumped in front of me. "I love your funny little English accent." She started chasing me across the dance floor.

"I can't. I've got to leave soon." I was desperately searching for Max. We'd made the curfew deal.

"Pete, I'm going." I pulled the mask of the top of my head. "I've got to get back to the ship. I think Max left already." Pete and Nadia were snuggling on a couch near the DJ box.

"I'd come with you, but I think I'm in there with Nadia. You understand, don't you?" Pete reasoned. "Head straight out of the bar, then second left across the bridge, then the ship is right there."

I needed to lose the crazy lady and find Max, so I made a sharp exit when she wasn't looking. I climbed out the secret staircase and through the upstairs bar, and finally I was back outside. The snow had stopped and had turned to ice so I was skidding along like Bambi.

I turned a corner and suddenly it went incredibly black. I was in some sort of maze following its twists and turns, expecting the ship to come into view. It began to get darker and darker along the path. I could just about make out that the walls were etched with images of naked women. The music from the clubs had faded

away. I was walking in total silence, wondering where I'd turned
wrong when,

SPLASH!

I was completely soaked from head to foot. I looked above into
the night sky to find a very well-built woman with huge frizzy hair.
She was dressed in nothing but a transparent negligee, balancing
on top of a ladder, holding an empty bucket. I looked at the woman
in disbelief; this bitch had just chucked ice water over me!

She began shouting in German and waving her fist at me. I
panicked and ran as fast as I could out the maze dripping wet. When
I finally escaped back out onto the main street, the passersby were
laughing and shaking their heads at me. Then the penny slowly
dropped: I'd taken the first left. That was the forbidden area the
taxi driver warned us about.

"You don't go down there." A guy scolded me on the street.
"The ladies think you're trying to steal their business." He pointed
back into the darkness where I could still hear the German
woman's rants.

The snow started lightly again as I was making my way over
the bridge, picturing myself being found in a pile of snow by the
roadside, frozen to death.

I'd almost made it across when I spotted a figure in the distance
coming towards me. I could make out a tall outline amidst all
the snowfall. I prayed it wasn't the German Jack the Ripper or an
escapee from a nearby mental asylum. That was all I needed.

I turned back and shouted to an imaginary Max: "Hurry up.
I've been looking for you everywhere," hoping that whoever was
approaching would think I had company and therefore would not
mutilate me. It was so cold, I had little icicles forming on my nose
from the drenching, and my hair was turning to soggy cardboard.
Not a good look.

The figure was getting closer and closer. I could just about make
out who it was. Oh my word, it was him. The gorgeous guy from

the crew bar. He, of all people, was about to see me with frozen snot hanging from my nostrils. It was too late to compose myself, he was already right in front of my face.

"Are you ok?" he asked, looking rather alarmed. "You're from the ship right?" He was speaking to me. I thought I was going to faint.

"I'm fine, thanks. I'm just a bit cold." I didn't make any reference as to why I was soaked wet through, and neither did he. I tried to flick my hair flirtatiously, but my fringe was so iced over it hit me right back in the face.

"I'm just looking for the ship to get back home," I said casually. "I don't suppose you know where it is?"

"It's right behind me." He gestured towards the ship which was indeed right behind him. He looked away for a split second so it was a good time to knock the icicles off my nose. I was also trying to work out his accent to figure out where he was from, but my ear drums had frozen over. He definitely wasn't English.

"Oh, right, yes. I'll be headed that way then." I waved as I darted up the street, still sliding on the ice.

Great. My first proper encounter with the most handsome guy I'd ever seen and I looked like a drowned rat.

I eventually got back on board, in one piece with all limbs intact, albeit frozen over. I hurried back towards my cabin. I was very annoyed to find someone slumped asleep against my door. I assumed it was Lisa's ukulele player, but I could only see the back of the head. They were snoring so loudly, I prodded the sleeping body as hard as I could.

"Excuse me." I was so mad that this stranger was in my doorway.

"Bianca." Max jolted upright. "I'm so sorry. I got carried away. Then I ended up locked in the cloakroom with a guy dressed as Freddie Mercury."

"I thought you'd been kidnapped." I hugged him tightly. "I've just been ice bucketed by an angry prostitute on a stepladder."

"Wow. I thought my night was weird." Max hugged me back. "I'll have to crash here. I can't find my key."

CHAPTER FOUR
The Law Of The Sea

DATE: 10 JANUARY 1998
DAY AT SEA
EN ROUTE TO NEW YORK, NEW YORK
CRUISING THE ATLANTIC OCEAN

I woke up feeling a little rough around the edges, to say the least. I was surprised to find Max curled up like a cat at the end of my bed, then it all came back to me.

"Don't be making a habit of that, mate." Lisa had her hands on her hips as she stood over my bed, looking very annoyed that Max had slept over.

"It won't happen again, I promise," I reassured her as she left the cabin for work.

I really liked Lisa so far. The last thing I wanted to do was piss her off.

"Max, wake up." I shook him gently. "I'm meeting Captain Cooper this morning."

"Why am I in your cabin?" He looked bewildered. "Was that cute dancer I like there last night? Did I make an embarrassment of myself?"

"The only dancer there was Nadia. I found you asleep outside my room. Not entirely sure how you got here." I checked my alarm. "We better get ready for work."

I stood up and quickly sat back down. The ship's rocking was making me queasy. The waves were crashing and thrashing against my little porthole. It was so rough out there.

"Don't worry, this is standard crossing weather when we do the tranny." Max yawned. "It'll get a bit rockier as the day goes on."

"What's a tranny?"

"It's transatlantic crossing. When we head over to the states from Southampton via the North Atlantic. Hour back, hour back, hour back each night till we get there."

There was a knock on the door. It was Maddie, looking bright-eyed, bushy-tailed, and as glamorous as ever.

"Put the kettle on, Bianca. It's about time we gave you some ground rules on the law of the sea," Max continued.

"Have you told her about the hour-back parties all this cruise?" Maddie asked Max. "There'll be one every night, so take your pick: an extra hour to sleep or an extra hour to party."

"Let's ease her in gently, Maddie." Max smiled.

I perched on the edge of my bed, trying to hide that the ship's movement was making me feel like I was swishing around in a washing machine.

"Now you've had time to settle in a little bit, we need to lay it out there and educate you on how to survive life on board." Max looked very serious. "Last night was fun, but we never, ever speak of what goes on the night before."

"But why?" I asked. "We weren't doing any harm." If anything, I could've been frozen over into a block of ice out there from the ice bucket.

"There's a saying on board 'every night is a Friday night and every morning is a Monday morning'," Maddie explained. "You can party as much as you like but you must turn up to your work duties the next day come rain or shine. If you don't, you'll get a warning or get fired."

That's why they were telling me after the big party night.

"If you drink, do it in moderation. If you go back to a cabin party, don't get caught. There are parties almost every night, you just have to be very careful not to draw attention to yourself. Otherwise you'll be tracked down by the 'Hit Squad' and you'll be sent home packing."

The 'Hit Squad'? I was envisioning a pack of gangsters strutting through the crew corridors smoking cigars and firing tommy guns.

"The Hit Squad are night patrol. If they see you tipsy or partying after hours, they'll report you up to the bridge and Captain Cooper has to send you home for disturbing the peace."

What? I could not be sent home. This didn't sound like much fun.

"We've lost many friends and colleagues along the way. It's so sad. If they get you, you're a goner," Max added. "So no matter what we get up to, what time we arrive home, or where we go at night, we never mention any of it on board."

"But I'm not the captain steering the ship!" This all seemed a little far-fetched. "This wasn't mentioned in my ship training."

"Doesn't matter. The rules are set and we have to abide by them." Max nodded. "It's a double-edged sword. Enjoy your free time, but be careful."

"When I first joined, three of my closest pals were musicians, and they were ALL fired at the same time for being in a cabin party. They were only drinking port and listening to Beethoven," Maddie recalled. "It was brutal. They were in the wrong place at the wrong time and sent packing home all the way from Sydney. They lost their jobs and had to fork out thousands for their flight home."

This was horrible. You couldn't coop people up in a confined space for months on end, then punish them for letting their hair down and having a party. Especially without giving the crew rest days. Ship life was a seven day week.

"You can party like it's Friday any night of the week, just be up, bright and breezy the next morning, every morning," Max said. "Stick to those rules and you'll be fine. It's worked so far for us, hasn't it Maddie?"

"It certainly has. Stick with us, girl, we're sly old sea dogs." She winked. "I brought you this to help you."

Maddie handed me a little blue book entitled 'Ship Terminology'. A pocket guide to help me with all this new ship speak. Port, starboard, forward, and aft were the only things I'd come to understand so far. This was exactly what I needed.

"Let's go for breakfast," Maddie suggested. "You two must be starving after last night."

Breakfast was served in the Officer's Mess, Deck Three Forward. Maddie's little dictionary was coming in handy already.

NAUTICAL TERM: OFFICER'S MESS - AN AREA WHERE SHIP'S OFFICERS EAT AND USE FOR RECREATIONAL PURPOSES

For my first couple of days, I'd been living on a stash of cereal that my nana had packed for me. So, this was my first dining experience sitting on red velvet chairs at a table laden with all the glass and silverware. Only the more senior crew on the ship got to eat here, like the captain and the chief engineers. I got to choose from an array of fresh fruits, granola, croissants, and more. I felt like a passenger.

"The food's not like this for everyone." Maddie tucked into her breakfast. "There's a crew mess below decks and all they serve is fish heads and rice."

It sounded gross; I couldn't contemplate eating fish heads.

"Day one into a fairly smooth crossing with only a matter of days to the Big Apple!" Max gave us a narrative.

"I've never been." I smiled. "I can't wait to see it."

"Oh you'll love it. Sightseeing, shopping, cocktails. We're going to have a blast. Have you felt sea sick yet?" Maddie asked.

"Not one bit," I was pleased to announce as the rocking from earlier had died down.

We made our way down to Deck One Forward crew area, the same level as my and Lisa's cabin.

NAUTICAL TERM: AFT - THE BACK OF THE SHIP

This book was helping me no end. I could just about get my bearings with this newfound information.

A huge green corridor stretched as far as the eye could see, running from one end of the ship to the other. It felt like rush hour at the tube station as there was so much human traffic, people lugging cases on trollies, trays upon trays of food being transported, burly-looking ladies screaming orders down walkie talkies, wheelchairs and walking sticks being dragged in every direction. I was dodging people coming towards me, they weren't slowing down for anyone. It was like Piccadilly Circus.

"Why's everyone so manic?" I asked. "Are they going to miss something?"

"This is the pace of ship life." Max jumped out of a bell boy's way. "It's all go, every day. Guests come first, they need to be served 24/7 and pronto."

"They call this corridor the M-1 because of the traffic." Maddie opened a big steel door leading off the walkway. "First stop, Crew Mess."

NAUTICAL TERM: CREW MESS - AN AREA WHERE SHIP'S NON SENIOR PERSONNEL EAT OR USE FOR RECREATIONAL PURPOSES

This was the total opposite to the Officer's Mess. It was very basic and really cold inside, kitted out with rows upon rows of grey plastic chairs and tables. It was packed with crew eating breakfast. The smell in there was getting right up my nose.

"What the hell's that smell?" I covered my nose until I started getting strange looks from the crew eating the food with said smell.

Maddie led me around the corner to the food aisle and there they were, troughs and troughs of fish heads and rice. Dozens of fish eyes staring up at me. It was quite disturbing. There was also the occasional dish of pale-looking vegetables.

"We get that nice food just up two decks and everyone else eats this?" I felt rather guilty that we got the better end of the deal.

"Be thankful, girl. We both had to eat in here until we got promoted." Maddie creased up her face in disgust. "We've done our time."

The other doors off the M-1 led to the crew laundry, the crew gym, a crew library and another secret route to the crew bar.

"Oh, there's plenty do here. That's if Cynthia ever gives you any time off." Maddie laughed. "Gotta go and do a manicure, I'll catch you later."

Next was the big trip up to the Bridge.

NAUTICAL TERM: BRIDGE - WHEELHOUSE WHERE CAPTAIN AND OFFICERS NAVIGATE THE SHIP'S COURSE

My little book was really coming in handy, I was becoming more sailor-like by the minute.

Max and I took the elevator up to Deck Twelve and passed through two heavily-coded doors rigged with lots of security cameras.

"Captain Cooper." Max buzzed on the telecom. "I'm chaperoning Cynthia's new secretary for her bridge visit."

"Send her in," a very well-spoken voice answered back.

The bridge doors opened and we were greeted with floor to ceiling views of the never-ending North Atlantic sea. There wasn't an inch of land in sight.

In the centre of the room, there was a huge space ship style control panel, and bleeping sounds came from all different directions.

Two of the bridge officers had their backs to us and were busy mapping out on a huge chart. They had yet to notice our arrival. One was really tall and the other was quite short.

"There he is." Max nudged me really hard in my rib. "The guy from the crew bar that you liked."

"You're joking." I felt my cheeks burning red. He looked so handsome in his uniform, even if I was only looking at the back of his head.

"Oh, look who's here." The smaller guy noticed. "It's the famous weather girl."

Both of them spun around to meet Max and I. I couldn't look him in the eye, so I started babbling on to the smaller one.

"It's lovely to finally meet you, Captain." I awkwardly curtsied like I was meeting the Queen, then put my hand out to shake his. He looked so young for a captain.

"Oh, I'm not the captain. I'm the third officer of the watch, James Sussex." He laughed with a very cut glass English accent. "This is our first officer of the watch, Davide Martinez. Let me go and let the captain know you're here,"

So that was his name. He even sounded like a film star.

NAUTICAL TERM: OFFICER OF THE WATCH - A DECK OFFICER ASSIGNED TO WATCH KEEPING AND NAVIGATION DUTY ON THE SHIP'S BRIDGE

I'd turned from red to a deeper shade of purple, firstly mistaking the captain, and secondly, I had to officially shake Davide's hand. He didn't look much like a Davide, but he did look even more amazing in his uniform and stripes. I still couldn't speak.

Max could see my embarrassment, so began to make small talk with him before I managed to get any words out. He just smiled dreamily the whole time.

"Miss Drake." The captain strode out of his office and shook my hand tightly. "Great to have you on board."

I quickly pulled myself together. "It's lovely to be here, Captain Cooper. I'm very excited to get started."

The captain was of tall, slim build with the thickest grey moustache and eyebrows I'd ever seen. He wouldn't have looked out of place riding a penny farthing in the 1800s.

"Well, we're very pleased to have you. As I'm sure you're already aware, myself and Cynthia have very high standards. Lady Anne is of the highest calibre and we expect all our ship's company to represent that." The captain spun round to his officers. "Well, will one of you give Miss Drake a tour then?"

"I'll do it!" The smaller guy jumped in. Phew. I couldn't have coped if it was Officer Davide.

James gave me a tour of the bridge, explaining the different controls, what did what, what to press when, and eventually ending up out on the crow's nest looking out to sea through a pair of binoculars.

NAUTICAL TERM: CROW'S NEST - THE MOST OPTIMAL VIEW FOR LOOK OUT TO SPOT APPROACHING HAZARDS.

"So, what do you think?" James asked. "Do you fancy a job up here on the bridge?" He leant in a little too closely as he took the binoculars from me.

"I'd need a lot more training to work up here." I sat on the desk, edging away from the over-friendliness.

"So, first time at sea then, Bianca?"

"Yes, it's all totally new to me. I'm learning a lot."

"I've been watching you on the morning show," he admitted. "I have to say, you do have quite the face for television. Very pretty."

"Thanks for watching. I'm glad you think so." I was being as short as possible, trying to avoid where he was going with the conversation.

"I come from a family of musical theatre directors, so there's not a lot I don't know about performing arts."

"So you're a singing sailor then?"

"You could say that. I'd be more than willing to help you settle in. How about dinner one night?" He was right up in my face again. "I can help you be more specific for your weather reports, being a bridge officer and all." He laughed at his own comments.

I was put on the spot, I daren't say no.

"Ok, I'll take you up on that," I hastily agreed. "I can't say when, though, as I've a very busy schedule."

"On that subject, how's it going having the dragon as a boss?" James pulled a face. "She's been at sea forever."

"All good, when she's not breathing fire. The forked tongue doesn't help. What does this switch do?" I quickly changed the subject and pointed to a multitude of buttons.

"That's connected to the PA system for the ship's announcements." He quickly pulled me away from the ledge I was resting against. "And you were just sitting on the microphone switch." The colour drained from his face.

"What do you mean? What have I done?" I panicked.

"I think you've just broadcast our conversation through the entire ship's public address system."

"Are you joking?" I felt light-headed and broke out in a sweat.

"The old man's not going to be happy." James pointed to Captain Cooper behind us, seemingly oblivious. "Just carry on like nothing has happened. I'll let you know if it went through the tannoy."

I took that as my cue to leave, terrified at the thought of Cynthia hearing the fork-tongued comment. Out of the hundreds of buttons in that room, of course I had to go and sit on the loud speaker activation.

"My team chuckle over the weather report on the morning shift," the captain laughed. "Jolly good show. Keep it going." Phew, he certainly hadn't heard anything over the microphones then.

Max and I said our goodbyes and left the bridge.

"Well, that was awkward," Max teased as soon as we got outside. "You really fancy Davide don't you? Trouble is, looks like the other fella is after you now instead."

"No he wasn't. He was just being friendly, wasn't he?"

I was trying to act as nonchalant as possible, masking the fact I was dying inside at the prospect of the whole ship hearing me being chatted up. And can I also add, by someone that I didn't fancy in the slightest.

"Oh Bianca, you're so naive. I definitely think your man likes you too, but he's just a lot shyer than little James."

"Do you think so? I mean, all those officers watch the weather!" I said out loud before back-tracking. "I mean, I'm not bothered, Max. I'm too busy,"

"We'll see about that." Max smirked.

Max and I got back to the office where a pretty amused-looking Pete was busy working away. He quickly stopped what he was doing as I sat down at my desk.

"Bianca, I've just got to come out with it," he blurted out after a few seconds of silence. "Have you just been up to the bridge?"

"Yes." I gulped, knowing what was coming next.

"I've just heard through the PA a conversation between you and one of the officer's asking you on a date."

"No! Did it come through there?" I asked pointing to the speaker in the corner.

"Yep, not just through there, through most of the crew quarters. Even the dragon part."

I dropped my pen and looked at Pete in horror. Max kept quiet and tried to make himself look busy by messing around in the filing cabinet.

"Oh my god! What am I going to do?" That dizzy feeling returned.

"Well, I took the initiative to find out that Cynthia was in the spa having a facial when the conversation came through. She didn't hear it, but most of the crew did. I'm sure it'll only be a matter of time before she gets wind of it."

"Bloody hell, Bianca. What happened up there?" Max asked. "I didn't see anything and I was up there with you the whole time."

"James was asking me on a date and mentioned that Cynthia was a dragon, so I said she had a forked tongue whilst I was leaning on the speaker activation."

"Jesus Christ, Bianca. That could only happen to you." Max looked just as alarmed as me. "I think you should go own up to Cynthia straight away and tell her it was all in jest."

"I think you should leave this one to me," Pete suggested. "Just keep a low profile after work."

I took Pete's advice and went back to my cabin, worrying myself into oblivion about what the next day would bring.

When I got back, Lisa had left me a written message by the telephone to call Officer James up on the bridge. Reluctantly, I called him back.

"Bianca, I'm afraid everyone knows about our date." He guffawed. "Don't worry, Captain Cooper eventually found it funny, however, the same won't be said for your boss."

"Don't even joke, I'm going to be strung up."

"Well, darling, it will be the both of us she strings up, as I was the instigator." He didn't seem at all bothered. "Let me know when the pretty little weather girl is free for dinner."

CHAPTER FIVE

New York, New York!

DATE:17 JANUARY 1998

PORT OF CALL: NEW YORK, NEW YORK

ARRIVAL: 8.00AM

OVERNIGHT STAY: (ALL ABOARD 6.00PM 18 JANUARY)

NAUTICAL TERM OF THE DAY: PORT SIDE - LEFT HAND SIDE

It was finally here. The day I'd been waiting for my entire life. Lady Anne was docking in New York City.

Wide awake at the crack of dawn, I was crouched on the window ledge, peering through the porthole, but all I could see was dark grey clouds and the tips of the waves.

"This view is awful. It's so grey outside," I wailed to Lisa.

I grabbed my coat and ran up to the crew area on deck five to catch a glimpse of the sail in. I was one of a few who'd made it up there so early, all of them snapping away with their cameras.

"How's your new boyfriend?" One of the bar waiters smirked.

"Boyfriend?" The realisation of the PA system conversation quickly crept up on me. Word really got around on these ships fast. I ignored the comment, choosing to take in the whole New York city sail-in moment stress free.

It was slightly foggy in the early morning light, yet I could just about make out Lady Liberty herself, standing tall and defiant just like I'd seen in the movies. It was breathtaking, a sight I'll never forget. The mist began to clear as we sailed under the bridge towards the Hell's Kitchen dock area. And then it came into view. The Manhattan skyline in all it's full glory. Dozens of iconic buildings, tall and beautiful against the waterfront.

"Ladies and gentlemen. Welcome to New York City," the captain came over the PA. "Can all guests please make your way to Deck Two, to be cleared to go ashore."

I ran back to the office early to get a head start with work.

"Morning, Bianca," Pete smiled. "Look, I spoke to Cynthia about the PA system."

Before he'd even finished his sentence, my pager started to buzz. I jumped out my skin. That thing scared the life out of me. It was time to face the music, so I reluctantly knocked next door.

"Planning on going out today?" Cynthia's raspy tones echoed out into the corridor.

"I was hoping to go out, if you didn't mind," I asked very sheepishly. "I've never been to America." I prayed she wouldn't make me stay on board.

"Well, after the embarrassment of my assistant being chatted up for the whole ship's crew to hear, you should count your lucky stars you're still onboard."

"I'm so sorry, Cynthia. I really didn't mean it." I looked down to the floor.

"Seriously, they're all going to think the weather girl is a floozy, flaunting herself in front of all the officers." She shook her head. "There's no denying who it was either, with your accent."

"If I go on the dinner with him, it will be out of sheer politeness." She put up her hand to cut me off.

"We've a very important celebrity guest arriving here in New York that I need you to look after." My heart sank. "She's arriving tomorrow, therefore I'll allow you to go ashore, but not until later this evening when your work is complete. Make sure you're available to chaperone our VIP guest early in the morning. Do I make myself clear?" Her voice rang through my ears.

"Of course. Thank you so much, Cynthia." I was elated. I could not wait to experience my first stop in the United States.

"Pete, I've still got my job AND I can go out tonight!" I skipped back into the office safely out of Cynthia's ear shot. "Maybe Cynthia's not so bad after all."

"This is the passenger list of all new joiners in NYC." Pete put the folders on my desk. "We've a dozen VIP guests that we need to be prepared for. We've even got a Lord sailing with us. Only the finest calibre guests for Lady Anne."

By 6.00pm all of my work was done. Max, Maddie, and I were ready to go ashore. The three of us walked arm in arm wrapped up against the cold. Block by block we crossed, and it wasn't long before the bright lights and billboards of Times Square came up ahead of us. I couldn't contain my excitement any longer. I was running to get there, then all of a sudden I was right in the thick of it.

It was just like I imagined, but a hundred times better. The huge billboards, the show posters, Radio City Hall, the MTV Studio, the Broadway box office. I was finally in Times Square. My dream had come true.

There was every store you could think of on the most gigantic scale, but there was no time for shopping, so we headed over to Central Park to check out the ice skating rink.

Central Park was the biggest I'd ever seen in my life. We got lost inside trying to find the right directions. The snow-kissed trees were so pretty in the January weather, every now and then we would spot a horse trotting around in a winter coat making it into even more of a picture postcard.

"I can't believe we're here. It's so beautiful,"

"Ah, girl, you should see the place in the summer. People everywhere, all the hot yanks with their tops off," Maddie winked.

Finally, the ice rink came into view. I hadn't been on roller-boots (never mind skates) since my primary school days and even then I wasn't very good.

"Just before we go in, you should be aware I'm probably going to be a liability on the ice." I hinted to Max and Maddie to keep one hand for me.

Sure enough, my first time ice skating was a bit of a disaster. When I wasn't holding onto my new friends for dear life. screeching with my eyes shut, I was holding on to the sides and dragging myself around like a staggering old drunk. In between the stress of trying to stand up and skate, I kept reminding myself how magical it was to be skating here in Central Park.

Max was a natural, so confident and light on his feet, making it look so easy. I plucked up the courage to do a little solo skate, just a small one in a straight line over to the exit.

I didn't see the little girl skating next to me. She wasn't at my eye level. She must have been about four or five, and I tripped right over her, arse over tit. She came away unscathed, whereas I was in a big heap in the middle of the floor.

"I'm so sorry. I didn't mean to hurt you," I apologised.

"How about you learn how to skate before you put those boots on, Lady?" The little girl retorted, brushing down her clothes, sounding about twenty years older than she was. That told me, then.

"Bloody hell, girl. You're a disaster." Maddie quickly came to my rescue and escorted me off the ice to safety. We made a sharp exit before the girl's parents came to kill us. Well, me, specifically. We decided to call it quits and headed for a cocktail at a nearby hotel bar overlooking the park from the twelfth floor.

"Cheers to New York." Max toasted with his martini. "Short and sweet, but you finally got to see it, Bianca."

"It was fantastic. Thanks so much for showing me around. This place is perfect to end it in." I reclined in the comfy bar chair.

"End it? Are you joking? It's only early. We're going right over to this really cool roof-top bar I know!" Maddie exclaimed.

A little voice in my head reminded me of the earlier run-in I had with Cynthia. I was about to do the sensible thing and have an early night, when the little devil on my shoulder got the better of me. Who was I kidding? I wasn't going to miss my first night out on the tiles in New York for anything.

We hailed a yellow taxi to Maddie's venue and queued outside in the freezing cold. There were people queuing for almost a block up the street.

"Get your ID cards or passports out now please," the door-men shouted.

"I'm so glad they don't do this back home, otherwise my bar-crawling career would've never began at age fifteen," Max shouted as they checked our IDs.

The bar was very plush inside, with a white grand piano at the bottom of a huge twisting staircase. We climbed the stairs to the rooftop part of the bar. The cold air hit us as it blew through the glass patio doors.

"We get these cute little coats to keep warm." Maddie passed us little hooded fluffy capes that reminded me of Red Riding Hood.

There were lots of the ship's crew already up there: bar staff, waiters, chefs, musicians, singers and dancers. Some of them I'd never even seen before. We gathered around a long black table on high stools all wrapped up in those little cosy get ups.

"We've got a good group going here," Maddie whispered. "Plus I wanted you to meet my new fancy fella. He's a chef from Paris."

Maddie introduced Max and I to a very shy-looking guy who looked smitten with her.

"I'd like to propose a toast." One of the dancers stood up and cleared his throat. "I'm thrilled to be here tonight in New York City and I'm very excited to be on this wonderful journey sailing around the world with you all. CHEERS SHIP MATES!"

We clinked our glasses and cheered to the voyage we were about to embark on and to new friendships.

"Bianca, I just love him. His name is Serge," Max confessed, referring to the dancer who'd just made the toast. "I'm sure he aimed that speech just at me. I'm going over to chat to him." He was all starry-eyed.

As Max was busy chatting up Serge and Maddie was getting very cosy with the chef, I began to feel like the spare wheel. I did wonder if any of the bridge officers would randomly turn up. It would've been nice to accidentally bump into that guy. But there was no sign of anyone from his department.

As I began chatting to more of the ship's crew, the cocktails and conversations flowed.

"We heard your announcement yesterday, with the guy asking you on a date," Nadia, Pete's dancer friend, confessed. "We were worried for you that Cynthia would be mad."

"You know, she wasn't too bad. I think she's beginning to like me." I rolled my eyes.

Nadia introduced me to all of her dance troupe. They were all totally gorgeous and super friendly.

"We love your weather reports every morning." One of the dancers laughed. "Very entertaining."

I couldn't believe people actually thought I was any good. I had no idea so many people on board watched it.

After a couple of Manhattan cocktails later, I sensibly decided it was best to go back to the ship.

"Me and Jean-Francois are going to China Town for some spring rolls," Maddie winked. "I'll see you tomorrow."

Maddie linked arms with the chef and made her way out of the bar.

"Max, I need to go. I have to meet the VIP in the morning."

"Okay, I'm coming. I'm getting nowhere fast." Max looked dismayed. "Maybe I'm just not his type."

"Or maybe you just need to play it a bit cooler," I encouraged. "Come on, let's go."

As we got to the bottom of the staircase, I spotted a huge stuffed tiger poised in full attack mode with teeth and everything, posing next to the unattended piano. What a photo opportunity, I thought.

"Max, get a picture of me lying on top of the tiger." I giggled in my tipsy state.

"Are you sure that'll hold your weight?" Max laughed. "Go on then."

I dived on the tiger's back almost like a sky diver jumps out of a plane, thinking about what a great picture I was going to get.

CRASH!

No sooner had the camera flash clicked then the tiger's legs cracked and gave way with me on top of it. I smashed to the floor, sprawled out on top of the rubble. I'd snapped all four legs with my weight and managed to twist my own knee in a knot. I felt rather faint.

"The doormen are coming." Max panicked.

"I need to hide." I dived off the wreckage and jumped behind a huge red curtain. I was holding my breath, terrified they'd catch me.

"It was some drunk guy. He just left that way," I heard Max explaining to the doormen.

My heart was racing. I never meant to smash it to smithereens. If they caught me, what if they charged me for animal cruelty?

"You can come out now, they've gone," Max hissed through the curtain. "Act cool."

I emerged from my hiding place and quickly scurried out of the bar. My knee was burning up. I was so scared I was going to be caught. We ran as fast as we could and jumped in the nearest taxi.

I went straight back to my cabin with an awful throbbing pain in my knee. Thank goodness the alcohol had numbed the pain slightly. I went out like a light as soon as my head hit the pillow.

CHAPTER SIX
Tiger Aftermath

DATE: 18 JANUARY 1998
PORT OF CALL: NEW YORK
ALL ABOARD: 6.00PM

NAUTICAL TERM OF THE DAY: STARBOARD - RIGHT HAND SIDE

I woke up the next morning just after dawn to prepare to meet Cynthia's VIP. I was not prepared for the state of my knee. It'd blown up like a balloon. I couldn't stand on it, let alone walk on it. I began sobbing with the pain.

"Mate, you're gonna need to call the nurse and get that seen to." Lisa looked concerned as she loaded me up with painkillers and gallons of water. "It looks twisted or sprained. Ring them now before it gets any worse."

"What do I tell Cynthia?" I wiped the tears from my eyes.

"How did it happen, mate?" Lisa asked.

When I told her what happened, she burst out laughing, which made me giggle, too. After all, it was ridiculous. I was crying in pain with one breath and laughing with the next. Lisa concocted a plan: I'd tell a little white lie and say I twisted my knee whilst skating at Central Park.

I didn't think Cynthia would take the whole 'pissed up on a roof top and jumping on a stuffed tiger' story very well. I called Max to get our stories straight before I called the medical centre.

Twenty minutes later, I was being transported out of my cabin in a wheelchair. My knee had gotten so swollen, I couldn't walk at all. The nurses took me for an X-ray and the results came back pretty quickly. It turned out, I'd sprained my knee quite badly and I'd need crutches to help me with walking.

I was devastated. I had my target on board and the VIP guest arriving. Cynthia was going to be furious. I confessed to the nurses my worry about my job and my boss.

"It's not like you did it on purpose, love. These things happen," the nurse reassured me (making me feel even guiltier). I was wheeled back to the cabin to sleep the painkillers off. The nurse advised me to have the full day off, but I couldn't. I had far too much to do.

I woke up a little while later feeling very woozy, but the pain had gone thanks to the medication. I had to get ready, but I just kept creasing up laughing at myself in the mirror. Those painkillers were really strong.

I soon sobered up when Cynthia rang to update me about the VIP arrival. I was meeting a celebrity author, 'Dr. Christine Riley' whom also had a famous TV show back in the day. I asked what she would be talking about.

I wish I hadn't. I was hoping she'd be discussing knitting or flower arranging. Christine's expertise was in fact, sex for the elderly. This lady was on board promoting her newest book title: Sex for the Over 70s.

It took me twice the normal amount of time to get to reception. I was about as good at coordinating these sticks as I was at ice skating. I spotted an elderly lady perched on the top of her luggage, reading from lots of papers.

"Excuse me, Dr. Riley?" I asked the little old lady.

"You must be Banca. Very nice to meet you. I've been waiting for you." She jumped off her case to shake my hand. I was too giddy to inform her my name had an 'I' in it, plus she was so little and cute.

"My dear, we must call a porter to help us," Christine exclaimed. "Whatever happened to you, dear? Let me guess, jumping from a wardrobe. Who's the lucky guy?"

I burst out laughing. "No, nothing like that. It was very icy yesterday and I had a skating accident," I explained. "I should be off these things in a few days."

The bellboy took the bags to the room as I chaperoned Christine up there. She was very bubbly and chatty, asking me about myself and telling me all about her new book (which was making me blush).

We got to her cabin, or I should say her suite. It was amazing - two tier with two living rooms, a four poster bed, floor-to-ceiling windows plus the services of a butler. The best VIP treatment Lady Anne had to offer.

We sat in the lounge whilst I ran through her celebrity speaker programme for the cruise, book signings, TV appearances, stage talks; it was quite a packed schedule.

"Have some chocolate, dear." Christine offered me some of her welcome hamper contents that I'd put together earlier. "You look a bit pale Banca. The sugar might help." She couldn't get my name right, so I decided to just go with Banca.

"Is Cynthia still here? You know, the lady who never smiles?" She winked.

"Yes, Cynthia's on board." I giggled. "I've no idea what you're talking about. She's always smiling."

It was time for me to film the weather slot, so I excused myself and hobbled up to the TV studio.

"Ladies and gentlemen, if you see me around the ship, limping on crutches, don't worry. I've a slight sprain in my knee due to the over excitement of New York." I winced in pain behind a false camera smile. "I decided to try out ice skating for the very first time and had a little accident. Let me know what you all got up to in NYC. I'd love to hear your stories. That's all from me, have a great day!"

I'd announced my version of events on camera. It was on film and would be broadcast to the whole ship the following morning. I had to stick to it.

When I got to the office, Pete already knew what happened as the nurse had been to inform Cynthia. I asked Pete how she took it.

"Quite well, considering. I think she's just thankful she still has her assistant here to look after Dr. Riley." He looked concerned. "Mrs. Riley is a full time job in itself, then you've your own job to do. If you need help with anything, let me know."

"I'm going to try and work as much as I can, Pete, but these painkillers are making me very drowsy," I mumbled.

The door swung open and Cynthia barged in, looking furious.

"Could you have picked a worse time to mess up your knee, Bianca? This is the start of a very important voyage and you decide to dislocate your ankle. Well, you're no good to anyone," Cynthia screeched.

I couldn't believe she was berating me in front of Pete. Tears began to well up, but I fought to keep them down.

"I'm sorry. It was an accident. This won't affect my job performance at all," I said quietly.

"Too bloody right it won't affect your performance, or you'll be on the next flight home," she barked as she slammed the door behind her.

I sat there horrified and humiliated. I continued my work in silence, trying not to cry. I tried not to let Cynthia get to me, but she was breaking me down little by little and I was about to crack.

For the first time since I embarked the ship, I felt like going home. I wanted to pack my bags and leave. I knew it was all my fault, but I hadn't hurt myself on purpose. Thank goodness Cynthia didn't know the real story behind my injury or I would've been dead meat.

"Do you think I could go back to my cabin for half an hour? The doctor said I had to keep my leg up as much as possible."

"Let me just check with next door." Pete went to Cynthia's office. He came back looking rather awkward.

"I'm sorry, Cynthia said you're to stay and improvise with the desk for your knee," Pete muttered. "She said to empty one of your desk drawers and rest your leg in that."

"I'm in pain here," I protested. Then I realised it wasn't a question, but more of an order. I cleared my second drawer out then rested my leg in it. It was so uncomfortable. I was legs akimbo and delirious from all the painkillers.

Much later on, back in my cabin after a lot of thought and unbearable pain, I decided to call my nana. I'd had just about enough.

"Bianca, you knew it was a big job when you took it on. Take it on the chin and get on with it," my nan advised. "How's your knee feeling? You're supposed to be working, not skating round like Torvill and Dean."

So I told my nana the skating story, too. Don't judge me.

Lisa had left me in alone for a night at the crew bar with her musician. I lay there feeling really sorry for myself when Max arrived with a cup of tea to cheer me up.

"Bianca, I'm so sorry. I heard about the desk drawer as a leg scaffold. It could've been a lot worse. You could've been locked up in a New York prison for criminal damage," Max said very matter of fact. "That poor tiger. You're lucky those doormen never caught you."

"Don't remind me. You know what? Today was the first time I've really felt like going home," I admitted.

"You can't go home." Max stroked my arm. "Maddie and I thought you would say that, so I got you a card." He pulled out a Get Well card out of his bag. I ripped it open and read it.

BIANCA DRAKE GET WELL SOON!
REASONS TO BE AN OLD SEA DOG!
1./ You can't leave me. I'm only just beginning to like you and you're almost as stylish as me therefore make me look good
2./ You need all the tips and advice from Dr. Riley as you can get!
3./ We've only just begun the most amazing world voyage
4./ Cynthia will get easier to deal with in time
5./ You haven't even spoken to the hottie yet (properly)
6./ Maddie will miss you - you're our third musketeer now
PLEASE DON'T GO ANYWHERE!

I smiled at all of those reasons. They were very valid. Max was right, I should stay and face the world head on. Besides, I was only just getting into the swing of things of this crazy ship life.

CHAPTER SEVEN
Sex For The Over 70's

DATE:19 JANUARY 1998

DAY AT SEA

EN ROUTE TO: PORT EVERGLADES, FLORIDA

CRUISING THE ATLANTIC OCEAN

NAUTICAL TERM OF THE DAY: STARBOARD - RIGHT HAND SIDE

I had the best night's sleep on those tablets. I woke up refreshed and ready for the day. Then I remembered I still had the crutches and the desk drawer to hang my leg **on.** Yet there was no time for self pity as I had a breakfast appointment with Christine at her suite.

"Come in dear. Do sit down," I was welcomed at the door. "I've ordered breakfast for two. The butler's bringing it up now. He's ever so nice. His name is Bentley, very British name, don't you think?"

"I don't want to get in trouble with Cynthia," was my immediate reaction. I couldn't be caught eating passenger food in the penthouse.

"Don't be silly, Banca. This is our little secret. This is a breakfast meeting." She winked at me.

We went over her lectures for the cruise, with the first one held that afternoon in the Grand Hall. Christine pre-warned me there was never an empty seat in the house when she spoke. She said the older generation knew her books and media persona very well and she had a big following.

"You're on the front page of the newsletter today." I passed Christine the copy over.

"You might want to put some extra staff on the theatre doors," she said as she sipped her tea.

Surely these talks wouldn't be that popular? These guests came on board to play shuffleboard and bridge. They didn't do things like that - did they?

It was 1.00pm and time to take Christine down to the Hall for her talk. Those crutches were really getting on my nerves; I couldn't get anywhere any faster than a snail's pace.

When I got to the venue, I was gobsmacked. The lobby was packed, with people coming from all directions. I ushered our VIP guest through the back stage door and closed the door tight behind me for the sound check.

"Banca! Have you seen them all? You'll have to open the doors soon before there's a riot," she shouted over the microphone.

"They're all here for your talk?" I was stunned.

"Yep, happens every time I do these ship gigs. I did tell you we'd need crowd control."

I called Cynthia to ask for more staff to help police the event. She gladly assisted. She seemed pleased that the talk had drummed up so much interest.

The crew arrived in force to help me deal with the sex-crazed crowd gathering outside. Max and a few musicians were sent down to help out. One of the musicians was really cute with big blue eyes.

I'd never seen him before, but there was no time to waste. I became all sergeant major like.

"Thanks for coming everyone," I shouted at the crew. "As you can see, we're hugely overcrowded in the main lobby and we need to clear the area as fast as possible."

It was like a military operation. The plan was to get the crowd in two orderly lines, one for port and one for starboard entrance. (See, I was learning!)

Then we would show each guest to their seat in a calm and orderly fashion.

I gulped as we got to the main foyer; there were so many guests and we had a maximum capacity to stick to. The doors opened and the crowds flooded in. The organisation had gone out the window, people were arguing over seats and pushing each other out the way. They were desperate to be as close to the stage as possible. You'd have thought Elvis was making a comeback.

Ten minutes of absolute chaos passed, then by some miracle, everybody was seated. There wasn't an empty seat in the house, plus gatherings of guests who insisted on standing at the back.

"Ladies and gentlemen, thank you so much for coming today." Christine came onstage to rapturous applause, bowing to the crowd. "Today, we're going to be discussing that very popular question. Should the over 70s still be having sex?" She put her ear out to the crowd. "Well, what do you think? Of course they should!"

The crowd cheered in agreement as Christine went into great detail about love when you're over the hill. The audience lapped it up. Some had brought notepads and were scribbling down every word she said.

"Now, I've only enough for the first two rows." One of the stage crew passed Christine a big bag of bananas. "Banca, dear." My face dropped. "Please, can you give these out to the ladies in the front?"

I took the bag and distributed them, thanking the heavens that was all I had to do. I'd a rough idea what was going to happen next, and wanted no part in it. Desperately trying to keep a straight face, I spotted Max hiding behind a pillar in hysterics.

Once the banana massage demonstration was over, it was time for the power point presentation of positions for people of a certain age.

I didn't know some of those diagrams were humanly possible. I had to twist my head a few times to get the right angle. The note-takers were now drawing out rough sketches. After a few slides on octogenarian Kamasutra, it was time for the question and answer session.

"Can you raise your hand if you have a question?" Christina asked.

"I'll go first!" A gentlemen shouted from the front. "I think I'm addicted to Viagra. Can you help?"

And with that, the questions began flowing in, covering everything from oysters, to swinging, to brothels.

Cynthia eventually had to come on stage to call time on the session, as we had run over schedule.

"Ladies and gentlemen, we'll be sure to schedule another opportunity to ask Christine. Can I kindly ask you to vacate the theatre? We next have our classical concert."

"Forget your classical concert," a lady shouted. "I want to know how to cure my husband's foot fetish!"

The audience booed Cynthia then clapped and cheered for Christina as she took her curtain call. I'd had quite enough sex tips to last me a lifetime, so I was waiting near the theatre exit for it to all end. I felt a tap on my shoulder and was pleasantly surprised to find the cute musician guy I spotted earlier.

"Hi," he whispered awkwardly.

"Hello, can I help you?" I whispered back.

"I'd like to invite you for a drink."

I was a bit surprised, but he was really cute, so I decided to hell with it.

"Sure, when?" I replied.

He looked very pleased. "Tomorrow night in the crew bar?" He had a very distinctive accent.

"Ok, what was your name?"

He whispered his name to me three times and I still couldn't make it out. The closest I got sounded very much like Raphael or Roberto, but a lot more like Ravioli, so that's what I decided to go with. When I repeated it back to him he seemed to respond to it. What harm would it do by meeting someone just for a cocktail?

Christine's thank you speeches drew to a close and it was time to man the doors as the guests left the theatre.

"Jolly good!"

"Very informative."

"Dr. Riley is a guru, an absolute genius."

Were just some of the compliments from the guests as they vacated the talk. I was so pleased they all enjoyed it.

I went straight up to film the weather report, but my knee began to throb again. I carried on regardless and was as chipper and cheery as I could be for the camera.

"Please remember to check your daily newsletter for the times and locations of Dr. Riley's book signing. It's sure to be a sell out," I told the camera.

I went back to the office to put my leg back in the drawer and got back to work. I was pleasantly surprised to find on my desk a huge plate of chocolate-covered strawberries with a little card that read:

'Dearest Banca,

Thank you for all your help today you did a wonderful job despite your injury. Keep smiling.

Love CR x'

Why couldn't Christine be my boss instead?

Still feeling slightly disturbed by that afternoon's talk, Max and Maddie and I met in the crew bar. Maddie was planning for the next day in port.

"Tomorrow we hit Florida. We can have a girlie day if you like?" Maddie asked. "I've been here a million times, so I'll think of something touristy for us to do."

"I'd love to. But right now, I really need to go to bed." I pointed to my walking aids.

"I can't go." Max looked deflated. "I'm working all day on the world cruise dinner plan for when we hit Sydney."

"We'll get you on a tour with the excursion office and they'll put us for free," Maddie said. "I'll pick the best one for us to do together."

"I didn't even know that was an option." I was immediately interested.

I left the bar to make my way home. As I was hobbling down the corridor to my cabin, I spotted him again: Officer Davide Martinez. The last time we bumped into each other like this was Hamburg, in the aftermath of me being swilled by a prostitute.

I pretended I didn't see him, which wasn't at all possible as the corridors were so narrow. I concentrated on the bottom of my crutches so I didn't have to look up and become embarrassed again.

"Hello, Miss." I almost pressed my crutches on his foot as he stopped right in front of me.

"Oh hello. I didn't see you there," I lied, looking up whilst trying to regain my balance.

"What happened to you?" He pointed to my leg.

I spluttered out the skating story, feeling a tiny pang of guilt as he looked quite concerned for me. He'd obviously missed the morning show when I spun my yarn.

"Well, I hope you get better, Miss." He smiled as he was walking away.

I smiled then let out a huge sigh of relief as he passed.

"You never told me your name up on the bridge?" He shouted back to me from down the corridor.

"It's Bianca. That's BEE-ANN-KA," I replied, beaming, totally over-excited that he actually wanted to know.

He smiled and waved me goodnight. I got back to the cabin with a huge grin on my face. He was the most handsome guy I'd ever seen, period. I was far too flustered to ask him anything. Anyhow, I had a sneaking suspicion I'd find out more soon enough.

CHAPTER EIGHT
Floridian Fiasco

DATE:21 JANUARY 1998
PORT OF CALL: PORT EVERGLADES, FLORIDA
ARRIVAL: 7.00AM
ALL ABOARD TIME: 4.00PM

BANG BANG BANG

I woke up to hammering on my door at the crack of dawn. I dragged myself to the door half asleep to find Maddie at the door.

"Sorry to wake you, but if we're getting off this tin can, we need to get to work early." She pointed to her watch which read 6.30am. "We need to sign up for the tour. I think we should go to Long Beach."

I got ready and attempted to walk unaided across the cabin, still aching, but I almost did it with a small hobble. That was good enough for me. No more hop along, and I was going to experience the Sunshine State for the first time.

"Are you sure you're going to be ok without those crutches?" Maddie looked a bit worried.

As soon as the clock hit 10.45am, we rushed to get ready to meet on the gangway. Maddie went to the crew office to get our immigration forms, which were needed to disembark the ship.

She brought mine down to the cabin. It was a flimsy piece of paper with my name on it that looked like a receipt.

"What do I need this for?" I put it in my purse.

"Just keep it with you. Everyone has to have one," Maddie advised. "I thought we could do some ship history today. We'll visit the sister ship of Lady Anne. She's called Lady Jane. She's retired now and they made her into a floating hotel. They do the best brunch."

We joined the guest tour, double-checked everyone was seated on the coach against the checklist, and made our way out to the port area.

We bought our tickets and began to explore, starting at the top deck, then working our way down. Lady Jane was so tiny in comparison to the Lady Anne. It was decorated very similar to our ship with all the original fittings. We went to the wheelhouse and visited the engine room. We saw a crew cabin from back in the day. It was a tiny space with four bunk beds inside. FOUR people in a cabin the same size of mine and Lisa's. I don't know how they did it. It was cramped enough with just two.

After our tour finished, we went to the brunch in the main dining hall. The food was out of this world: a very posh buffet style with every type of food you could imagine. We filled our plates up as much as we could then sat down with a glass of champagne under the biggest chandelier.

"Cheers, girl." We clinked glasses. "Thanks for a lovely morning. I'm glad we did this. It's nice to get a bit of history sometimes."

"Thanks so much for inviting me. It's been great." I smiled, sipping my drink.

"I stopped doing things like this, well, because I always used to be with my ex." Maddie pulled a face then laughed. "We can have lots of girly days, and with Max, of course. He's one of the girls, too."

We were chatting away and getting to know each other a bit better. Maddie seemed so well-travelled and independent compared to me.

Eventually, we got back onto the subject of her ex; Maddie was engaged to be married to a guy she met on the ship. They'd been together for three years and the wedding was booked.

"Last summer, my mam fell ill, so I went on emergency leave for a while. I left and everything was fine. I got back and he wouldn't talk to me, avoided me, ignored my calls. I was stunned." She took another sip of champagne. "I couldn't work out what I'd done wrong. Then I seen him with one of the pantry girls, and he confessed he'd been seeing her behind my back. He called off the engagement."

"Is he still on board now?" I was shocked. What an absolute horror.

"Yes, he's here. They both are. The girl's on vacation, so she'll be back. It was rough. I had to go back home to cancel the wedding, sell my dress, all alone. I nearly quit life at sea, but Max persuaded me not to." She sighed. "It was months ago now. I'm getting over it. What doesn't kill you makes you stronger, girl."

"You deserve much more than that, Maddie." I squeezed her hand.

I felt so bad for her. Boys on ships were ridiculous!

We strolled up to the cruise terminal arm in arm and joined the ship queue. We waited ten minutes before it was our turn for immigration.

"Immigration forms please," the officer said on the gangway.

We both began to rummage in our bags for the receipt of paper we were given that morning. Maddie passed hers to the guy. I was still looking; I searched my purse. It wasn't where I put it earlier.

'Don't panic Bianca' I told myself; it had to be there. I emptied every part of my purse and shook it, then I ransacked my handbag.

"Where is it?" The guy barked at me, looking very irritated.

I jumped out my skin. He was making me panic even more.

"I don't know. It was in my purse," I cried.

"Well, you keep looking at this side of the gate Ma'am." He pointed to the opposite side of the gate then told Maddie to go ahead and board the ship.

I was on the floor scrambling through my things. I had a sneaking suspicion that it may have fallen out when I got my purse out to pay for lunch. The officer let all the crew in the line on board and came back over to me.

The officer let all the crew in the line on board and came back over to me.

"Why did you disembark the ship without your proper papers, Miss?" He continued to shout at me.

"I didn't. I had it this morning, I promise."

He began to radio someone about a crew member breaking the immigration laws. Surely he wasn't talking about me?

I continued to check my bag, but it was no good. The piece of paper had gone. Suddenly, I was being escorted to a back room of the cruise terminal by two officers. I thought they were going to handcuff me.

"Can you please tell me what I've done? I think I might've lost the paper by accident. I'm sorry!"

"So you 'think you may have lost' it? Well that's just too convenient. Listen, Miss, if you don't have it, then wave your ship bye bye." He smirked, pointing to the ship in the background.

I thought he was joking. When then they started to take all my details: my name, my passport number, I realised how much trouble I was in.

"Please, I'm innocent. I didn't know the paper was so important," I pleaded, feeling like I'd just killed someone.

"Wave bye bye!" the officer repeated. He seemed to be really enjoying the fact that he was making a young and frightened girl upset. He left the room and locked the door behind him so I couldn't escape.

My nerves had gotten the better of me, so I began sobbing into my sleeve in the prison cell-like room on my own. I was in the middle of a port with no money or belongings and the ship was about to set sail without me. Why had no one told me how important that form was? I didn't even know what it was for!

Thirty minutes passed and I was imagining the reversed-charge phone call I would soon be making to my poor unsuspecting mother back home from Fort Lauderdale penitentiary.

The ship had fifteen minutes before it was due to set sail when out the window, I saw Maddie rushing down the gangway with Carl, the crew manager. They were talking with the immigration officers for what seemed like a lifetime whilst I was crying at them through the window.

"Come on, Bianca. You can board the ship on the basis that you must go to your cabin and double-check if the form is in there," Carl said, opening the locked door of my 'cell,' looking very serious.

I nodded, wiping my tears, but I knew it was no use looking in my room. I had it in my purse on the way out. I raced from the dock side to my cabin, blocking out the pain from my injured knee. I burst open the door and ransacked my room.

"It's no use. I know it's not here. What's going to happen? Am I holding the ship up?" I cried.

"Bianca, calm down. If it's lost, it's lost. Tell Carl. He'll deal with it," Lisa said.

I ran back to the gangway, relieved to find the doors already closed with Carl leaning against the wall.

"They've let us sail with a hefty fine. I better go up to the Captain and inform him." He sighed heavily. "This is not going to go down well at all."

I've never felt so relieved hearing the whirring of the ship engines leaving port. A few moments ago I was so close to being left ashore.

The second I got back to the cabin, the pager buzzed with Cynthia summoning me to her office immediately.

"The ship has been fined 4000 dollars for your total disregard towards the immigration procedures." Cynthia glared at me in disgust. I was squirming in my seat whilst holding back my tears.

"As a representative of this company, you've brought humiliation upon us to the immigration officials, at one of the biggest cruise ship terminals in the world. I hope you're proud of yourself." She continued, "Anything more from you, and you'll receive your first formal warning. May I remind you, you are in your probation period for the first three months and we can just as easily terminate your contract without notice."

I didn't have anything to say. I was mentally drained. I just nodded in agreement and left the office. I went outside to the open deck and sat down to watch the ocean and clear my mind.

It all seemed so unfair. I was new, for god's sake.

I wanted to hide away in my cabin, but then I remembered I had a date that night. The last thing I wanted to do was glam myself up and have a drink. Still, I didn't want to stand the guy up, so I took a deep breath, brushed myself down, and went to get ready.

"Who are you trying to impress, mate?" Lisa asked as I was dolling myself up.

"Well, promise you won't tell anyone?" Lisa agreed, so I told her as I applied my red lipstick (which somehow always ended up on my teeth).

"I'm meeting a guy for a drink. He plays in the band and his name is Ravioli. Well, that's what I think he said his name was."

With only had a slight tinge of pain in my leg, I could make my way up to the crew bar with a (very) slight limp. As I got there, Ravioli jumped out of his seat and greeted me with a big kiss on the cheek.

He went the bar as I took a seat in the corner. I was confused when he came back with just one drink. He just smiled and put his arm (awkwardly) around me and sipped his drink.

"I'll go and get myself a drink then, shall I?" I stomped over to the bar and ordered a vodka cranberry.

This wasn't off to a good start. He was too tight to buy me a drink when they were only $1 in the crew bar. Tight arse. I cleared my throat, took a deep breath, and tried to start a conversation.

"How was your day then?" I sat back down, vodka in hand.

"Yes, thank you," he replied, smiling sweetly.

His English didn't appear too fluent. After an awkward pause, I began to talk about my day and how lovely Lady Jane was, leaving out the deportation part. I waited for him to join in or tell me what his day was like, but he just sat there grinning and staring at me.

"Would you like another drink?" I volunteered.

I stood at the bar, buying us both a drink and wondering how to get out of this really awkward situation. I downed half my vodka, then took both drinks back to the table.

"You're very welcome," I quipped, even though he never thanked me.

"You very pretty, Bianca. Where do you come from?" he asked.

I was so pleased he'd begun to talk. I told him about my home town, my mum, my nana, when out of nowhere he began stroking my hair, then leaned in for a kiss. I don't mean a peck on the cheek; I mean a full on snog! I recoiled in horror and jumped up from the chair, hoping nobody else in the bar had seen.

This guy wasn't interested in a thing I had to say, but was still trying to make out with me in the middle of the crew bar? No thanks. I excused myself for the extra early start I had in the morning. He looked really disappointed.

I rushed back to my cabin as quickly as I could, took all my makeup off, and jumped into bed.

"How was it, mate?" Lisa asked.

"You don't wanna know, Lisa. Let's just say Ravioli is OFF THE MENU!"

CHAPTER NINE
Columbian Mojitos

DATE:25 JANUARY 1998
PORT OF CALL:CARTAGENA, COLOMBIA
ARRIVAL: 7.00AM
ALL ABOARD TIME: 4.00PM

Four days had passed since my immigration fiasco and I finally felt like it was safe to go off the ship again. I'd worked all the hours god sent and it was time for me to have an afternoon off in the home of Shakira: Columbia, South America.

We were docked in Cartegena, an old fishing village on Colombia's Caribbean coast. Pete, Max, Maddie, and I hitched a makeshift taxi/pick up truck down to the black sand beach.

"Max, be honest with me? I feel like I'm hobbling since I hurt my leg. Am I walking funny?"

"No, you're fine. It's all in your head," Max reassured me. I hoped my one night of drunken tiger abuse hadn't resulted in me having a lifelong limp.

We found the tiniest beach shack playing loud reggaeton tunes, so we pulled up chairs and began trying to decipher the Spanish cocktail menu. I ordered a very strong 'La Muerte Negra' mojito.

Whilst we were waiting for our food to arrive, Maddie and I went down to the water to catch some waves. I was wearing my brand new (ridiculously expensive) sunglasses and was posing for a picture in the water when CRASH! A huge wave hit me and dragged me under the tide. I thought that was it. Goodbye, it was nice knowing you.

After what seemed like a lifetime with me fighting for air, the tide finally released me. I gasped for air in desperation. I checked my head for my designer specs. Of course, they'd gone.

"So remember, ladies & gentlemen, tidal waves can take you by surprise. Do take care when swimming in the sea of these beautiful ports." I recounted my day trip to the camera, leaving out the mojito part. I didn't want the guests thinking I lost my glasses drunk. (I mean, me, tipsy? Never!)

As I left the TV studio, I could still feel the limp slightly as I walked. I was panicking that I'd done permanent damage to myself. I bumped into Max as I was walking back to the office. He was carrying a huge china ornament in his hands.

"Are you going on the Antiques Roadshow or something?" I asked, pointing to the old-fashioned casket.

"Ssssh, Bianca, she might hear you. It's Mr. Braithwaite's wife from cabin 3454," Max whispered.

"What's she doing in there? I mean... why are you carrying her ashes?"

"Mr. Braithwaite and his wife were both regular cruisers and he's fulfilling his wife's last request. Bittersweet."

Max said that at times, guests requested to have their loved ones ashes scattered at sea. As part of his job, Max organised the ceremonies with the family and the clergyman.

I told Max about my walking problem and did a little demonstration across the office.

"I couldn't see it yesterday," he said, "but you've definitely got a bit of a limp going on."

I sat down, considering whether to call the nurse, when the phone rang and Max got called out of the office.

"Max, you can't leave me with Mrs. Braithwaite." I pointed to the urn on his desk.

"Bianca, she was a sweet old dear, she won't harm you." He laughed. "You're such a drama queen!"

Off he went, leaving me alone in the office with the lady's ashes. Don't get me wrong, I know the dead can't hurt you, but it was really creeping me out. Every slight noise I heard, I was jumping out my skin. I couldn't concentrate, thinking about poor Mrs. Braithwaite. Maddie came in to say hi, just at the right time.

"Thank goodness you're here, I was about to run out." I nodded towards the direction of Mrs. Braithwaite.

"Oh that's nothing," Maddie scoffed. "I'd rather scatter ashes off the back off the ship than deal with Cynthia everyday."

We were giggling as the door swung open and in walked Cynthia. Speak of the devil, as they say.

"It's the first Captain's Cocktail reception of the voyage tomorrow night." She wrinkled her nose at me. "And your presence has been specifically requested. I wouldn't usually permit my secretary to attend, but as the request's from a guest, I'm obliged to agree. You do own a cocktail dress, don't you? Or a full length gown?" she questioned whilst looking me up and down.

"Of course I do, Cynthia." I was delighted. I hadn't overpacked for nothing after all. It felt like the wicked stepmother was inviting Cinderella to the ball.

"I've got a few, actually. I just haven't found the time to wear them in the evening." I was smiling like the Cheshire Cat.

"Well, if you managed your time better, then you'd find more opportunity to wear them. Dr. Riley requests for you to pick her up at 7.00pm tomorrow evening. Do NOT be late." She sashayed out of the office in her pink and purple crinoline number, complete with massive train. I don't know how she fitted through the door.

That was the first piece of nice news I had received from my boss since joining. Even if she did it through gritted teeth, this called for a drink.

"Maddie, shall we go the bar for one?"

"What a long day." Maddie poured me a glass of rose in the corner of the crew bar. "Have you got over your tidal wave yet?"

"Just about. Tell me how to behave at a cocktail party?" I was so excited. "What do we wear? What do we say?"

"Basically, get dressed up to the nines and mingle with the guests. You can have max two of the champagnes they give out, but never ever accept any canapés, even if the waiter offers you. Cynthia will do her nut in."

I got onto my worry about my leg and whether I should call the nurse.

"You do look a bit of peg-leg, girl," she said very matter-of-factly. "Maybe you did some serious damage. I'd ask for the crutches back."

"I'm going to go back to the nurse first thing." I hung my head on the table in exasperation when a moment of Eureka smacked me right in the face.

"Oh my word." I pointed down at my shoes. "There's nothing wrong with my leg - LOOK!" I removed my shoes and started waving them at a very bewildered Maddie.

"I'm such an idiot," I screamed all over the bar. "I've had odd shoes on all the time."

I put my high heels on the table to show what I was getting so excited about. My shoes were identical in colour, but were very different in heel size.

I'd brought two pairs of nude high heels with me and been wearing odd ones for days; one high and one short. No wonder I thought I had a limp, there was about two inches difference in them. I thanked the Lord I had not suffered permanent damage.

Ladies, never buy two pairs of the same colour high heels - it can cause major emotional and physical trauma.

"Bianca, you've lost the plot, girl. Wait till Max hears this one." She stopped laughing and the atmosphere quickly dropped.

"Can we swap seats?" Maddie looked rather agitated. We switched seats so I was facing the bar and she was facing the wall.

"My ex just walked in. I don't think he's seen us." She covered her face with her hair and lowered her head.

I was so curious to see who he was, the guy who'd treated her so awfully. All I could see was a group of guys at the bar, along with that weird Ravioli guy I'd met. He spotted me in the corner and we exchanged waves very awkwardly.

"I'll try not to look, but I'm dying to know who he is," I said, focusing on pouring another glass of wine.

"I'll look around quickly then tell you what he's wearing. I really don't want him to see me." She glanced around, then described him to me. "He is wearing a navy shirt. He's the cute one with the big blue eyes."

Oh no. Those words rang through my ears and my stomach hit the floor. This could not be happening!

Maddie's ex was the weird musician guy I'd met for a drink. I tried to act normal as possible whilst inside my nerves were shattered. She could never ever find out!

I felt awful that I'd gone on a date with my new friend's ex fiancé! And he kept making it obvious by winking at me across the room. Thank god she had her back to him. I made a sharp exit and headed back to my room. So, Ravioli was the little sneak who broke Maddie's heart. It was such a small world working on these ships.

CHAPTER TEN
Penguin Party

DATE:21 JANUARY 1998

DAY AT SEA

ENROUTE TO: ACAPULCO, MEXICO

CRUISING THE PACIFIC OCEAN

The next morning, on my desk was an envelope addressed to me. I ripped it open, expecting it to be an invitation to the Captain's Cocktails that night. Instead, a photograph of a penguin fell out with a small note stapled to it.

Dear Miss Weather Girl,

We would like to invite you to be an honorary 'Penguin' and become the newest member of our secret on-board society. Your initiation takes place today at 4.00pm in the upper level of 'Cha Cha Cha' nightclub. Looking forward to seeing you there.

The Penguins

P.S Once read, please destroy this note.

Penguins are adorable, but I didn't know if I actually wanted to become one. I wondered what the initiation ceremony would be. Would I have to dive overboard for fish? This job was getting stranger by the day.

I arrived at Deck Twelve to the on-board night club. All the blinds were down and a 'Private Function' sign was outside the door. I knocked on the door.

"You made it," an elderly man with bright white hair cheered. He put his hand out to lead me in.

"Here she is, everyone. As promised; our very own weather girl." He gently pushed me into the centre of the dance floor.

There was a huge round of applause as I faced a sea of faces, all looking very pleased to see me. I couldn't see any penguins, although everyone was dressed in black and white.

"Hello," I waved at the crowd, smiling nervously.

"We'd like to begin your initiation." The man grinned from ear to ear.

I was completely dumbfounded, but being centre stage with the spotlight on me, I'd no choice but to play along. Everybody looked so pleased to see me, I didn't want to spoil the fun. Even if I was about to join some kind of cult.

"Don't worry, dear. I'll demonstrate first and then you're next," the man said with a twinkle in his eye. "I'm Gary, by the way, the founder of the Penguins."

A silver bin was placed at the other end of the dance floor. Then a lady passed Gary a cuddly teddy Penguin, and the whole room began to clap. Gary put the Penguin in between his knees and began to attempt to walk, he (eventually) made his way from one side of the dance floor to the other. Once across, he dropped the penguin in the silver bin. The crowd went wild cheering and clapping.

"Now, Bianca, it's your turn." Gary clapped at me.

"Is that all I have to do?" I asked, trying to keep a straight face.

"You have an extra prop to carry. As you're our weather girl, we thought you should have an umbrella." He presented to me a pretty lace parasol.

I had to walk across the dance floor with a stuffed penguin whilst holding a parasol to the tune of the teddy bear's picnic. Easy peasy.

"You don't mind being filmed for your initiation, do you?" He pointed to the big camera lens now in my face.

"Oh no, not all." I waved into the camera, smiling through clenched teeth.

As if this whole scenario wasn't peculiar enough, someone somewhere would have video footage of this forever more, great. I got myself in to position with the parasol in one hand and the stuffed penguin squashed in between my knees.

Off I sauntered very slowly, swinging my legs in semi circles whilst trying to keep my knees together, being so careful not to drop the penguin and parasol. I'd only managed three steps and dropped the penguin. It was a lot more difficult than Gary made it look. I blamed my stilettos.

"Uh oh, try again. All the way to the bin without any casualties." He picked up the penguin off the floor and signalled for the sound guy to stop the music.

I took off my high heels, so I could get this debacle over and done with, and went barefoot for my next attempt. I tried again, got all the way to the bin and dropped it again about three steps too soon. I was sweating by this point. The pressure was getting to me. Almost like I was competing in some type of bloodsport.

"Third time lucky, dear." Gary led me back to the starting point.

This time I hitched my skirt up, so I had no shoes and no hemlines in the way, still holding the parasol and smiling sweetly for the cameras.

The crowd began to clap again as I moved as slowly as possible across the dance floor, trying not to drop this bloody penguin. I was a few steps away from the bin when I began to giggle in hysterics, then the whole room joined in laughing - this was so ridiculous it was untrue.

"You're almost there." Gary clapped encouragingly.

Three, two, one.

BOOM! I got it in; in your face, Mr. Penguin! I took a bow and left the dance floor to everyone's cheers. I'd actually accomplished it. A gold medal wouldn't have gone amiss. Gary took me over to the bar for some water.

"Thanks for doing that, Bianca." Gary told me about the Penguin club. "A couple of years ago, after my wife passed, I started this club for regular sailors like me who were solo travelling. Its grown and grown every cruise. I called it Penguins as you know they're the only animals who stay with one partner."

"That's such a nice idea. I'm sure your wife would be very proud of you."

"We hold daily Penguin meetings in the library and we all love the weather snippets, so it's only right you should become an honorary member." Gary presented me with a little penguin badge and certificate to confirm my initiation.

I made my goodbyes and rushed to my cabin to get ready for the cocktails. I had to be ready early and I hadn't even washed my hair.

Bentley the butler greeted me in Christine's suite with a glass of champagne.

"Thanks, Bentley, but I don't think I should. I'm on duty," I said, shaking my head.

"Don't be silly, dear. I insist," Christine said as the glass was pushed into my hand. "We must drink to a successful cruise together."

We clinked glasses and proposed a toast.

"Let's keep in touch after this, Banca. I'm going to send you a little gift from New York when I get back."

I was secretly hoping she would offer me a job as her personal assistant, then I could swan around New York every day and be free from the wrath of Cynthia.

We were standing in line waiting patiently outside the Grand Ballroom. Everyone was dressed immaculately. The men were very dapper in their tuxedos and dickie bows with the ladies dressed in full-length gowns of every colour. It was a very glamorous occasion. I was a little nervous to go inside, hoping I looked the part. As we got to the entrance, the captain greeted us at the door.

"Welcome to cocktails, Dr. Riley." He shook our hands. I did a little bow as if I was being greeted by royalty.

"Before you leave us, Christine, I'd very much appreciate a signed copy of that book we talked about." He winked as the photographer's flash bulbs went off for the formal picture. Even the captain wanted sex tips, and he was definitely pushing 70.

The ballroom was beautifully decorated with huge bows and streamers, with was a string section playing classical music on stage. The bar waiters were rushing around, serving drinks on silver trays in their white gloves. I felt like I had stepped back in time to another era.

"Let's go, Banca. Let's mingle amongst the guests." Christine put her hand out for mine and pulled me over to the dolphin ice sculptures which were adorned with canapés and fancy cocktails.

"Pick whatever you want." She pointed to all the food and drink.

"But I'm not a guest." I stood away from the displays, remembering what Maddie said about not eating.

"You're my guest and I want you to relax. You never get to do these nice parts of living at sea." She passed me a fancy puff pastry of some sort and a glass of fizz. I took a swig of the champagne and put the pastry in a napkin, too scared to eat it. We'd only been in the room for a few minutes when the crowd began to gather around Christine, asking for photos and autographs.

Whilst Christine was busy with her audience, I went for a little wander around the party, being extra careful not to tread on my gown or anyone else's. Long dresses and heels were not a good combination.

The party was full of the ship's officers, all in their full formal rig out, which even made the most ugly looking guy become reasonably handsome; it had to be the uniform thing.

"They finally let you off your leash then?" Max joked. "How's your first cocktail party?"

"It's very surreal. I don't feel like I belong here."

"Of course you do. You should be here more often, if only CLP wasn't so mean." Max glanced towards over to Cynthia, who had her back to us as she chatted to the guests.

"There's your friend from up on the bridge, Officer James," Max said.

This was awkward. We were in direct eye line of each other. For a second he looked like he was going to come over, but then he was distracted by some guests.

"Mildred, look who's here. It's that funny little girl off the weather show." A little old lady dressed like a flapper girl covered in pearls stopped me.

"So it is." Another lady dressed identically to the first one shook my hand. "We watch you every morning and I have to ask, is it real?"

Was what real? My hair, my teeth?

"Your accent? Do you really talk like that, or are you acting?" The little old lady waited in anticipation for my answer.

"Do you ladies think I'm acting when I do those reports?" I asked them as they looked at me silently. "Nope, I'm not acting. I'm afraid it is 100% me speaking like and acting like I do every day."

"Well, that's darling!" The pair began giggling and squealing amongst themselves.

"I'd like to introduce to you all my wonderful assistant on this cruise, the beautiful Banca Drake." Christina started clapping and so did everyone else in her little circle. More of the guests started to recognise me and tell me how much they liked my little bit on the TV show.

I loved that I cheered people up on their mornings at sea - it was fast becoming my favourite part of the job.

"Banca, there's someone that would like to meet you." Christine ushered me over to a group of officers.

"Very nice to meet you again, Miss Drake," James said. "Where've you been hiding?"

"I don't get out of the office much," I explained. "This is the first cocktail party for me."

"Then I insist you get out more. Come to dinner with me tomorrow evening," he suggested, raising his eyebrows. "I'll send you an invitation."

"Ok, that would be really nice," I answered, feeling a little flustered.

"Did you just set me up on a date?" I asked as we walked back over to the ice sculptures.

"Maybe," Christine laughed mischievously.

CHAPTER ELEVEN
Tequila Sunrise

DATE: 30 JANUARY 1998
PORT OF CALL: ACAPULCO, MEXICO
ARRIVAL: 7.00AM
ALL ABOARD: 5.00PM

"Don't forget, dear, let me know all the details of your date with the hunky officer." Dr. Christine squeezed me tightly as we said our goodbyes.

I waved her off the gangway as she left to catch her flight home. I felt quite sad. She'd been so nice to me for the short time she was on board.

There was no time to waste, as I had the time off to go and enjoy the beach in Mexico! I went to get my bag ready and hit the shore.

No sooner had we set foot off the ship than this cute little old man begged us to come to his bar off one of the side streets. When we told him we wanted a chill day on the beach, he seemed quite offended.

"The two beautiful ladies, I take you to the best tequila bar in town." He hooked his arms into mine and Maddie's and marched us through swing doors into his bar.

"You don't come to Mexico just for sunshine. You try the local culture and tequila." He shook a pair of maracas. "I can get you tequila, poncho, sombrero, ceviche, donkey - anything you want."

As there was no way I'd ever be able fit a donkey in my small cabin, we decided on a sombrero each and tequila. We passed our host a handful of dollars and he promised us an afternoon of Mexican delights.

"My name is Pacho, and this is my place."

The bar was tiny, big enough for three wooden tables with lots of brightly painted skulls across the walls. Pacho got behind the bar and poured us our first tequila.

"I bring for you sombrero and some maracas. You must try the best enchiladas in whole of Acapulco!" He shouted in Spanish to the cook in the kitchen. "Now, you drink. I come back."

Two shots of tequila each and the sombreros showed up. They were so big, they couldn't fit through the entrance doors.

"These were made from the hand." He passed them to us, looking very pleased with himself. "Present you this." Pacho gave us a gift of tequila with the real worm in it.

"I like it in here. Let's give the beach a miss." Max opened the tequila bottle for more shots. "I mean, we can go to the beach in Honolulu."

"Ok, let's stay here. It's so cosy and cute." Maddie gave us our hats to try on for size. "What's everyone wearing for the uniform swap party? I've got mine sorted, I'm going as a chef."

"I'm going as one of the dancers. Katie's lent me her leotard and tutu, so I'll be a ballerina," Max replied.

"Is this tonight?" I had no idea.

"The dancers come as the engineers in the big boiler suits, the spa therapists as bar waiters in the waistcoats with silver trays," Maddie explained. "It's so much fun."

It sounded pretty tame, not like my kind of fancy dress party.

"Er, let me think. You, Bianca should go as... a housekeeper."
Max jumped off his bar stool. "Yes, I can see it now. We can make
you a name badge and everything." He was clapping his hands,
very pleased with his suggestion.

"I suppose so," I half heartedly agreed.

I had to fit in my dinner with Officer James and a fancy dress
party in the same night. I hadn't told anyone about the dinner. I
daren't mention anything after my last dating disaster that turned
out to be Maddie's ex boyfriend; I was still traumatised by it.

The chef brought out a tray of Mexican delights: enchiladas,
burritos, and three frozen margaritas. We stuffed our faces on the
delicious Mexican cuisine whilst sipping on the cocktails. Three
courses later and the tequila had certainly gone to our heads.

Max threw his sombrero down on the floor.

"The floor's filthy." I tried to pick it up.

"Noooo, let's dance around the sombrero, like it's
your handbag."

Max was cheering and clapping as Maddie and I began to dance
around the hat to the loud Mexican music. Even Pacho and the chef
lady joined in. As Maddie was spinning Max across the bar floor,
the doors swung open and in walked Ravioli arm in arm with one
of the shop girls off the ship.

Maddie's dance moves came to a halt and she removed her
sombrero hat very quickly. Ravioli greeted us all, then deliberately
sat on the table opposite us. He kept winking at me when no one
was watching. My nerves were gone.

"I think it's safe to say the fiesta is over," Maddie scowled.
"Let's go."

We thanked Pacho and the chef, grabbed our hats, and said
our adios.

The fresh air hit as we got outside.

"Time to sober up," Maddie advised, and pulled a litre of water out of her bag. "So he's got two girls on the ship now, the pantry girl and a shoppie." She shook her head.

"Don't even look at him," I advised. "Look right through him. He'll get his karma one day."

It was just a five minute walk back to the ship. We showed our passes and headed through the security gate in the port.

"I think we better take off the hats." Maddie folded hers and tucked it under her arm. We got across the gangway, a little tiddly, and tried to walk as straight as possible.

Max went first through the check point, shaking his maracas and shouting 'Arriba, Arriba'.

"Please put all items through the bag scanner, including those." The security man pointed to Maddie's sombrero.

I rolled my hat as small as I could and tried to squeeze it through the bag scanner, but it kept bouncing back into shape. I was trying to refold it when my wristwatch got caught on the stitching, and I couldn't free myself from it. To my horror, the belt began moving forward, taking my arm with it.

"Help me, Maddie!" I shrieked as my arm was being dragged into the machine. I was now half way on the belt, about to go head first into the X-ray machine. The security guy ripped my watch off right in the nick of time.

"Thanks so much." I tried to shake his hand to thank him, but he stepped away from me. He was furious.

"You could've had an arm off there. You bloody entertainment team!"

My pager started bleeping as soon as I got back on board.

"Hello, Miss Weather Girl." It was James. "It's me, officer of the watch. Listen, I can't make tonight. I'll be up on the bridge with the old man. We're expecting a bit of rough weather. Maybe tomorrow?"

That suited me. I could check out what the party was all about. Max and I raced to the office to catch up with work.

"Can you tell me where you've both been all afternoon?" Cynthia barged in the office looking rather pissed off.

"We've just been to the beach, Cynthia." I shuffled my papers and desperately tried to look busy.

I didn't want to give away any signs of our tequila tasting afternoon. It probably didn't help that Max was at his desk typing away with his huge sombrero on.

"Maxwell, take that ridiculous looking hat off and grow up."

She stormed out the office just as quick as she entered in my imaginary swirl of black smoke. I swear I could hear vultures in the background.

"Why don't we go down to the uniform locker and get your housekeeping outfit?" Max quickly changed the subject.

"Not bad, mate, not bad," Lisa said, checking me out in our cabin mirror.

I had the full outfit: the dress, the apron, the rubber gloves, even a feather duster - I was ready to go. Lisa was dressing up as the ship's nurse with scrubs, a stethoscope, and everything. If you ever decide to get a job on a ship, pack some fancy dress costumes; ship people love a good costume party.

Lisa had been AWOL for a few days. She'd been sleeping out almost every night since she hooked up with that ukulele guy.

"I feel a bit nervous rocking up to the crew bar dressed like this." I adjusted my apron for the fifth time. "I don't really know that many people yet."

"Have a shot of this, mate, you'll be right." She poured me a shot of neon green liqueur. "Rule Number One: Never go to a costume party sober."

The crew bar was absolutely packed. We had to fight our way to the bar. Max's tutu kept getting in the way of everyone, whilst Maddie looked hysterical in her chef whites, complete with a two foot hat and a false moustache.

This was my first proper crew party and I was impressed. The bar was decorated with balloons, the music was pumping, and everybody was ready to party. The bar waiters were dressed as the shop staff, the deck officers were dressed as spa girls complete with hair and make up, the chefs were dressed as the security team; the whole ship's crew got involved.

Max did an impromptu ballet routine, pirouetting to the delight of everyone cheering around him. He pointed over to the other end of the bar and was mouthing something to me over the music, I followed his direction and he was pointing to that guy, Davide, the fit one.

What was it with this bloke? I never see him and he finally shows up whilst I'm dressed like an old washer woman. I pretended I didn't see him, but there he was, dressed in casual clothes, probably too good-looking and cool to participate in the fancy dress.

The best costume had to go to the Sergiy the dancer, who came as... wait for it...Cynthia! He'd had his makeup done, with an outlandish pink gown with a perfectly coiffed wig and obligatory pearls. He even had her sneer down to a tee. The party was in full swing.

I went to the bar to get another drink, squeezing through the gap to get served, when someone pulled my feather duster from my belt behind me.

"Excuse me, give me that back." I spun around. I couldn't believe it, it was Davide, waving my feather duster in my face

"Hello, Bianca."

He actually remembered my name. I tried to play it cool. I was nowhere near as tipsy as he was. I smiled and grabbed the duster off him and put it back in my belt.

"Would you like a drink, Miss Bianca?" I was buzzing inside and keeping cool on the outside.

"No thank you, I'm fine. I'm buying for my friends, too." I made my excuses and walked away.

I was kicking myself. Why didn't I just stay and chat to him? I couldn't relax in his company. I had a major, major crush on him.

"We're going to the dancers' cabins for a Russian vodka party!" Max announced.

"I'm not coming, love. I've got an early start." Maddie said her goodnights and left.

I also didn't want to go anywhere else. I liked it in the bar, but Max was so excited that the dancer guy invited him. I couldn't let him go alone. As a good wingman and friend, I agreed reluctantly.

Typical, the first time we'd an opportunity to talk and I was too bloody shy and far too sober.

"Na Zdorovie." We clinked glasses, packed like sardines into a tiny bunk bed cabin. I downed my shot of vodka quickly. Everyone looked at me surprised.

"No, no, no! You must do the Russian way," Sergey said. "Watch and learn."

Holding a piece of bread, he began to sniff it really deeply then tilted his heads back and downed the shot, then again another sniff to the bread, then randomly ate a pickle out of a glass jar placed on the shelf.

I was all for adapting to other people's cultures, but there was no way I was ruining a good vodka by munching on a pickle. Yak!

"It's ok. I'll know for next time." I really didn't want to feel rough the next morning.

The Russian music was blaring, complete with silver disco ball spinning from the ceiling. The door was constantly opening with more drunken revellers from the crew bar arriving. There were people everywhere: on the bunk beds, outside in the corridor, some were even squared inside the shower base smoking through the air vent shaft.

Max was outside trying his best to learn Russian from his dancer man, concentrating with a beer in his hand and still dressed in a tutu.

A grumpy security guard came down to the corridor and told us to lower the music otherwise he'd send us all home. Just as I was contemplating whether to leave, my decision was rapidly made for me when I spotted Ravioli making his way down the corridor.

"Max, I have to go. Have a great time. I'll call you in the morning." I raced down the corridor, but it was impossible to avoid him. He was heading straight towards me.

"Why you have not seen me again?" He asked, looking rather upset.

"I er, I have a boyfriend and you have a girlfriend. I can't see you again." I shook my head.

"Oh, but you will see me again." He smirked and walked off. This guy was a total sleaze. I wondered what Maddie ever saw in him.

The music from the party was turned up again full blast, whilst more crew brushed past me en route to the party cabin with bottles in hand.

The security dude was making his way back down to the corridor as I was heading up to my room. He radioed on his walk talky. "Assistance please. Hit Squad Alert, After hours party."

The dreaded Hit Squad. I made myself scarce as quickly as possible.

CHAPTER TWELVE
San Fran

DATE:4 FEBRUARY 1998
PORT OF CALL: SAN FRANCISCO,CALIFORNIA
ARRIVAL: 6.00AM
ALL ABOARD: 9.00PM

"I'm assigning to you to a group of guests that are boarding the ship today." Cynthia sipped from her coffee mug. It was 6.00am and she'd called me out of bed.

When I answered the phone I thought the ship was in a state of emergency. It sounded so urgent that I threw my uniform over my pyjama top and ran straight upstairs.

"Of course, Cynthia. When will they arrive?" I breathed a huge sigh of relief.

"A band of musicians are embarking from San Francisco all the way to Australia. They're using the ship to move all their instruments to their next concert." She rubbed her forehead. "They're some kind of folk band and there are thirteen of them." She looked horrified.

Thirteen hippie musicians from San Fran travelling with us all the way to Oz. It sounded very interesting.

Cynthia didn't want them disturbing the peace amongst our elderly guests, so my job was to welcome them on board and check in with them every day.

"Of course, Cynthia. I'll keep everything under control, don't worry." I gathered my notebook and quickly left to get dressed properly. We were just about to dock in the port of San Francisco and I could hardly contain my excitement.

"Union Square, Fisherman's Wharf, and the Castro, they're our top three," Max said, ruffling the map. "We have to go to Alcatraz." Max, Serge, and I stood outside the ship terminal deciding where to go.

I was tagging along with Max and Serge for the day with five whole hours to explore San Fran. All I was missing was flowers in my hair.

I wanted to visit Haight Ashbury, but it wasn't my day out to choose. Our first stop was Union Square.

We were taking pictures of the Dewey Monument when loud music began playing across the square. It was so loud I couldn't hear what Max was saying right next to me.

"I can't hear you." I put my fingers in my ears.

A huge crowd of people gathered right next to us, all frozen in different positions as if they were about to bust a move, when Michael Jackson's 'Smooth Criminal' began pumping out the speakers. Max pulled me away from the crowd jumping up and down animatedly.

"MJ Flash Mob!" he said, mid high-fiving Serge. "Unless you can moon walk, stay over there."

Serge joined in and followed the medley with the dozens of people dancing in time. Max looked even more in awe than ever of him. I loved San Francisco already!

"We need to head to Fisherman's Wharf to get to Alcatraz."
Max studied his map. "We'll catch a tram, the only way to travel
in San Fran."

"How very Mrs. Doubtfire." I clapped my hands together.

"Who?" Serge looked confused.

We were strolling around the Castro area, in and out of all the
side streets. There were lots of Victorian style houses painted in
pretty pastel colours. It was really cute.

"Max, look what we have over there." Sergey pointed across
the street. "Let's take a peek."

Over the road was 'Sydney's Sex Store'. They both looked very
excited. Slightly apprehensive, I followed them inside.

It was very dark in the store with all manner of strange looking
devices on the shelves. I didn't know what half of them were for.
Max and Sergey were giggling away like a couple of school kids.
I was wandering alone down an aisle of what looked like blow up
donkeys when...

"OUUUUTTTTTTTTT!"

Screamed a really tall guy dressed in a very risqué all leather
get-up from his bottomless chaps to his train driver cap. I had
no idea who this man was shouting at, so I pretended to carry on
shopping, then he shouted again and pointed in my direction.

"You! Woman! OUT!" He was staring at me like he wanted to
kill me. My stomach flipped. "No women. Men only."

He marched towards me and pulled me out the shop by my
arm. I looked at Max and Sergey for help, but they were too busy
giggling and did nothing to help me.

As I was pushed outside, the guy made a hissing noise at me
then stormed back into the shop. I was gobsmacked. I'd just been

thrown out of a sex shop. That was definitely one I couldn't tell my nana about.

"Thanks for helping me. Some friends you are," I fumed at the boys furiously when they finally rolled out of the shop.

We went for a rose in a fancy street cafe over the road to try and make me feel better about the situation.

"That was so embarrassing!" I muttered.

"Nos'drovia." Sergey proposed a toast. "To Sydney's Sex Shop."

"What did you buy?" I tried to peer through his plastic bag.

"Ask me no questions and I'll tell you no lies." Max laughed.

An old battered VW camper van pulled up at the cruise terminal and out poured a group of long-haired and bearded men. I was waiting on the gangway to meet them. They were a little late, so I ran over to help with their bags.

"Hi, I'm Bianca. So pleased to meet you." I held out my hand to the first person I came to. "I'll be your point of contact for your cruise."

"Hey, Bianca, I'm Skye. Listen, sorry we're late. We kind of lost a drum kit along the way," He itched his incredibly long dreadlocks.

They began loading up their equipment onto the trollies, introducing themselves.

"Rain."

"Jep."

"Ziggy."

I was never going to remember all of them. They looked like they were playing at Glastonbury, not sailing on the grand old Lady Anne.

I escorted them to their cabins on deck 5. When I informed them of the no smoking policy in the cabin, they didn't look very impressed.

"We might have a jamming session tonight. Is that cool with you?" Skye asked.

"There's karaoke on tonight in the pub. If you want to do a few numbers after that finishes, I'm sure that would go down well." Their first night on board and I'd already arranged an impromptu concert.

I rushed back to my cabin to get ready for my dinner date with Officer James.

"Good Evening, Bianca. You look great." James was all dressed in white with his stripes on his shoulders and his hat. He took my hand and kissed the back of it just like in the old fashioned movies. "Shall we?"

There was a table laid out on the open deck under the stars with a bottle on ice and a bouquet of flowers. I felt quite taken aback. He'd pulled out all the stops.

We sat down to dinner and the waiter popped open the champagne. I was nervous, very nervous. I didn't know what I was going to talk about at a sit down meal with a very posh officer. I swigged the champagne as fast as I could.

"So tell me, what's your story? How did you end up on this magnificent vessel?" He leaned in to listen to my fascinating story.

Oh shit. I hated questions like that, almost as much as that other dreaded question 'Where do you see yourself in five years time?' I liked to think I would be too busy enjoying myself to even notice.

I didn't want to tell him the truth. I'd got bored in my little village and I was scared of getting stuck there for life so I ran for the hills. Instead, I spun a more exotic version about me working on a local newspaper and my passion for travel and journalism inspiring me to seek out a more adventurous life at sea.

"So, how about you?" I bounced the question back.

"I come from a long line of master mariners. My father and my father's father before him." He burst into an awkward laugh. "I'm surprised you hadn't heard of me before you got on board." He guffawed at his own joke.

Twenty minutes and an amuse bouche later, I learnt how his parents had their very own family crest and how his grandfather owned a castle back home. He certainly loved to talk and his specialist subject: himself.

"What do you like to do for fun?" He wiped the sides of his mouth with the napkin.

I was beginning to feel more like I was on a bloody job interview than a date.

"I like street dancing, yoga, and I love going to see live music." I hoped those answers were good enough. My dancing was in fact limited to this one break dance move I learnt in year nine, which often made a comeback after a couple of vinos.

"Music? Oh I love a good musical, don't you?" He looked over his shoulder, then whispered over the table to me. "Keep this to yourself, but if you ever want a free ticket to see CATS! I'm your man."

I expected another awkward laugh to follow, but he was serious. I actually meant I was more into getting muddy at festivals and going live gigs.

"I mean, I can't tell you who my connection is, but let's just say we're very good friends from the Rotary Club and he has an L and a W in his surname." He chuckled, slapping his own leg.

Oh god, this guy really was a lot posher than I could ever have imagined.

"I do love a good fundraiser, don't you? I do a lot for charity back home." He looked very pleased with himself. "My father and I hold an annual polo match for various causes."

Polo? The only polo I had ever encountered came in packets and tasted of mint. I was impressed that he did a lot for charity. I was less impressed that he was bragging about it.

By the time the main course arrived, I'd figured out the continual smiling and nodding was all I needed to do to look engaged. James' personality was a bit of a let down, egotism isn't exactly the most attractive quality.

As we were ordering dessert, my pager bleeped. I ran to the nearest telephone. For the first time, I actually hoped it was Cynthia kicking off down the phone so I could make my excuses and leave.

"This is Sam from the Golden Dragon on Deck 3. Please, can you come down to the pub? There's a bit of a disagreement over the karaoke." The waiter sounded a little distressed.

Skye and his band! I'd let them loose on karaoke night without a second thought, exactly what Cynthia was dreading. I went white, dropped the phone, and ran down to the pub.

"Give me that!" A little old granny was pulling the mike from Skye. "I was just about to do my song."

"Sorry, ma'am, we're going to jam for you all." Skye pulled it from the lady's grip.

The crowd of guests were booing and hissing at the band. Oh dear! I was going to get the blame for all this again.

"I'm sorry, I did say that after karaoke had finished you could do a few numbers, not interrupt it," I quickly intervened.

"If we have to listen to 'My Way' one more time, I'll jump overboard," Skye protested.

The little old granny pulled the mike back again then Skye retaliated and pulled it back. They began playing tug of war with the microphone wire. I covered my eyes. I couldn't believe what I was seeing.

"Don't worry, we called Pete," Sam told me. "He's on his way."

CHAPTER THIRTEEN
Aloha Hawaii!

DATE:9 FEBRUARY 1998

PORT OF CALL: HONOLULU, HAWAII

ARRIVAL: 6.00AM

ALL ABOARD:OVERNIGHT STAY (3.00PM THE FOLLOWING AFTERNOON)

Aloha Hawaii!

I managed to get off the ship nice and early without any delays. Maddie, Pete, and I had hired a Jeep convertible to go cruising around Honolulu, no less. Very swanky!

"Let's do a little test drive before we head off." I turned out of the car park and took a wrong turn straight onto a very busy highway. First time driving an automatic, never mind the driving on the other side of the road part. My feet were not familiar with the pedals and instead of hitting the accelerator I kept hitting the brake. We were bunny hopping down one of the most busy freeways in Honolulu and I was about to get us killed.

"I thought you had a driving license!" Maddie screamed, covering her eyes.

"I do!" The cars were honking me as I was blocking the road, speeding past us at 100 kilometres an hour. It was terrifying.

I saw the chance to exit the highway on the left and stopped at the nearest possible opportunity in a supermarket car park.

"What the hell just happened? Are you ok?" Maddie jumped out of the Jeep.

"Of course I have a driving license," I protested. "But I've never driven abroad." I got out to stretch my legs after the white knuckle ride.

"Well, didn't that occur to you before you volunteered to be our chauffeur around Honolulu for the day?" Maddie laughed.

"I'll be fine. I just need to do a little test drive. How was I to know that rental place backed onto a highway?" I shook my head.

"I don't fancy dying today, Bianca." Pete pulled his map out. "We want to get to Pearl Harbour in one piece, please."

I let those two fight over who had the best map directions and began my test drive round the car park, thanking god it was relatively empty. I didn't want to cause a pile up - it was only 9.00am. I just couldn't get the hang of the pedals, whatever happened to driving a car was like driving a bike? Actually, I wasn't a very good cyclist, either. I needed stabilisers till I was ten.

After a few minutes, I got my confidence back up. I just had to keep my wits about me regarding the wrong side of the road bits.

"Let's get this show on the road." I began pulling the roof off and putting it in the trunk. "Next stop, Pearl Harbour."

Honolulu was not the idyllic paradise I'd imagined in my head. It was very built up and there were a LOT of highways. There was everything here: shopping Malls, fast food joints, Walmarts, everything you would find in a big American city.

"Can't wait for Waikiki Beach!" I told my passengers, both of whom were very tightly strapped in and grimacing in terror.

Pete was my navigator, with a tourist map on his lap which was so big he couldn't see over the top. Maddie was in the back posing in her huge sunglasses. We were finally en route to explore. I just had to remember to keep on the right side of the road which looked like the wrong side to me.

We hit the road to Pearl Harbour. By that point I was doing less bunny hopping, but still struggling with Pete's directions. We were seeing the signs for Pearl Harbour, but kept missing the turns.

"Here's another sign for it! Turn now!" Maddie shouted from the back seat.

"There's too many cars in the way. I'm in the wrong lane!" I began to panic and completely missed the turn. "I'm sorry! I don't know where the hell I'm going."

We carried on down the highway. We got to the next turnoff, then got back on the highway again and headed back to where we started.

"I didn't expect my day of sight seeing to be from the inside of a car," Maddie grumbled.

"Oh, I'm sorry. Do you want to drive then, love?" I snapped. "I'm quite sure you can't, because you don't drive."

She snarled at me in the rear view mirror. I ignored it. I had to concentrate.

I was so close to the turn off, but I missed it AGAIN because I was in the wrong lane AGAIN!

We passed straight down the highway and past the memorial for the fourth time. I began screaming like a crazed lunatic at the top of my lungs, driving in the slowest lane of the freeway. Maddie joined in and so did Pete, which eventually turned into hysterical fits of laughter.

"I can't take this anymore, you guys. I'm so sorry. I knew we should've gone whale watching." I turned off at the next available stop and pulled into a petrol station. We agreed driving was too stressful and that none of us knew the roads well enough, so we headed back to the rental place and parked the Jeep up.

I was very happy to be hitching a taxi to the famous Waikiki Beach to check out the surf. I used to read about Waikiki in the encyclopaedia's in my nan's loft when I was a little girl and there I actually was, in Honululu!

We jumped out the taxi and crossed the grass to the beach. It was beautiful. It wasn't very wide, yet stretched on for miles with lots of surfers riding the waves.

"This is something I never thought I'd see in a million years." I dipped my feet into the warm blue sea.

"Check us out guys, day off on Waikiki beach!" Pete pulled his camera out and started taking photos.

"Why don't we try and bunk in one of them?" Maddie pointed to one of the luxury resorts along the beach.

We walked into the swankiest hotel along the strip.

"Watch and learn." Maddie strutted up to the reception desk like she owned it.

"Good afternoon." She put on her poshest English accent. "I'm the hotel manager on board Her Majesty's ship Lady Anne. Myself and my colleagues would like a hotel tour and possibly use of your pool facilities."

The receptionist listened intently.

"We can take you on a tour around the resort, show you our master suites, infinity pools, sample our a la carte lunch menu, then you can swim in our Olympic size swimming pool and use our swim up bar."

We all nodded eagerly. The ship name dropping had worked.

"That will be 140 dollars per person. Cash or credit?"

Ok, Maddie's idea hadn't worked, but still it sounded like so much fun we paid it anyway.

"Maybe next time I'll pretend I'm Cynthia," Maddie muttered under her breath.

We toured the golf course in a buggy, viewed the bedroom suites, ate a Hawaiian themed lunch, then it was time to sunbathe and chill at the pool. All the while Maddie kept up the pretence of being the hotel manager, but at times she forgot and went back into her thick Irish accent.

We threw on our swimsuits and dived in, straight over to the swim up bar for a Mai Tai cocktail. We waited patiently for our drinks to be mixed by a very handsome, long-haired bartender.

"Oh my god!" Maddie whispered in my ear. "He's gorgeous."

The guy was tall and tanned with light brown long hair and brown eyes.

"Where are you guys from?" The bartender asked, flipping our glasses up in the air like a scene from Cocktail.

"We're all from the UK," Maddie answered. "I'm (ahem) the hotel manager on one of the cruise ships that is in port today."

Pete and I had to stifle our laughter.

"Oh cool! I've always wondered what it was like to work on one of them." He flashed a smile. "My name's Daniel. I'm actually from Sydney. I'm just here for the season."

When we told him we were en route to Australia, he gave us tips on where to party in Sydney. Him and Maddie seemed to be getting on like a house on fire, so Pete and I decided to go for a little swim and leave them to it.

"This is what makes it all worthwhile," Pete said as we looked out onto the sea. "We work like dogs, but when the rewards are days off in Hawaii, can we really complain?"

I whole heartedly agreed.

"I know she gives you a rough time, especially." This was the first time Pete had opened up to me properly. "Don't take it personal. I've seen it happen so many times to the poor girl who ends up in your job. Unfortunately you are her dogsbody and that's just the way it is."

I appreciated Pete's honesty. If Cynthia was the price I had to pay in return for travelling the world and meeting all these amazing people, then so be it - you have to take the rough with the smooth and all that.

We swam back to order another Mai Tai. Maddie and Daniel were laughing and joking at the bar. I don't think she'd even noticed we'd been gone.

"Hey guys, Daniel's going to this really cool party on the beach tonight. No tourists, just locals. Shall we go?" Maddie smiled innocently whilst kicking me under the water, still holding together the English accent.

"Ok, sounds great! We're here till tomorrow, so why not? You only live once." Pete put his drink up in the air for a toast.

"Yes, let's go! As long as we don't miss the ship!" I said as we clinked glasses.

"Are you sure we should be doing this?" I asked Maddie as we were waiting on the pier for Daniel to pick us up.

"We're going to have the best night. Don't worry," Maddie said, putting another coat of pink lipstick on. "Plus you made us bring our handsome chaperones."

Max and Pete met us outside dressed in all white linen shirts and shorts. They looked so cute. I made sure all four of us went. Safety in numbers and all that.

A battered old red estate car spluttered into the car park and squeaked up to the curb, with Daniel waving very enthusiastically out of the window.

"Hey guys!" He jumped out to greet us. "So glad you could make it. You ladies look stunning." He kissed Maddie on the hand. I didn't get a look in.

"First, up we will go to this little Surf Shack, Sebastian's, then we'll take it from there. So we're going to be a little bit out of town."

Those words made me nervous. I already had visions of us having to swim back to the ship.

"It's a good job I brought along a few refreshments for the journey." Max handed out plastic cups and filled up our glasses with a very well hidden bottle of rose wine that was strapped under his trousers.

"Here's to a Hawaiian adventure!" Maddie put her arm round me. "We're going to have a great night."

Half an hour later, we got out at the tiny beach bar built out of old surfboards next to a small wooden dock, packed out with surfer dudes drinking beer and smoking.

"Hey, dudes, these are my ship friends I met this avo." Daniel introduced us to some of the locals. I could see Maddie was going weak at the knees every time he spoke.

Daniel went the bar to get us some drinks. I found it hard to balance on the chairs which were made out of bits of old surfboards and ended up on my backside in the sand for most of the time. Our host came back balancing a bucket of beers and a bottle of wine.

"I didn't know what you prefer, so I got both." He put the drinks on the table and cracked open a beer. "This is where all the workers hang out. You don't get any tourists down here - we like it that way."

He smacked me on the back. "Have you told these guys where we're taking them tonight, mate?"

Daniel told us were going over the water in a dingy to a tiny private island for a full moon party. I thought those type of parties only happened in Thailand, but apparently not.

We finished our drinks and got in the little boats to take us over a small channel of water. Maddie, Max, Pete, Daniel and I filled the last little rubber boat as we crossed the water.

We pulled up at another little wooden dock. I was last out and had to get hoisted out by Daniel.

"You really don't need clod hoppers for a beach party Bianca!" Max teased. "Take them off."

I removed my perfectly colour co-ordinated shoes and (begrudgingly) went barefoot. We passed some giant rocks and found a huge fire pit circled with people. Everyone was covered in neon face paint, a few were dressed in Hawaiian head gear and costumes. They were serving drinks out of a giant ice cooler whilst an acoustic band played in the background. I spotted a fire juggler near the water with a small crowd gathering round.

"Welcome to your first full moon party." We cheered, passing us each a cold beer. I took the drink and sat on the beach next to Max and Pete.

"Bianca, will you relax?" Max asked. "Don't worry - we're only staying for a few."

I couldn't help it. The ship was so far away.

"I'm the one who should be worrying," Pete continued. "If we don't get back on time, Cynthia will blame me before you."

"Oh Christ! We have only been here five minutes."

Max pointed over to Maddie locking lips with Daniel about five metres away.

"Ah, leave her. She probably needs it after the way that horrible guy treated her," I reasoned.

The fire juggler finished the show and come over to introduce herself to us. She was really pretty with huge flowers in her hair.

"Listen, I heard you guys are off Her Majesty's ship. I was wondering if you guys could put me in touch with your boss. Maybe I could get a gig at your theatre?"

I was just about to say I don't think a sexy six packed fire eater was appropriate for our guests (especially the old blokes) when Pete chipped in.

"I might just work closely with the person you need to know."

I should have known, Pete's tongue was hanging out and this was a perfect opportunity to use his job on board to help him get the girl. She seemed delighted and perched herself next to him to get more details.

"Shall we take a walk, Max?" I suggested.

What between Maddie snogging the face of Daniel and Pete drooling over the fire eater, it was time for Max and I to make a sharp exit.

We sat by the fire pit and got chatting to the guys around it. Some of them local, some of them backpackers.

"I'm just going to get us another refreshment."

Max made his way over to the cooler. I wanted to look the part for the full moon so I paid the face painter to do my face with luminous stars and moons. Time passed and I began to worry where the hell Max had gone.

Just as I was about to start a search party, Max turned up covered in face paints with a bright green wig on and large sunglasses shaped like coconuts.

"Max where have you been?" I asked. "And where are our drinks?" I asked as I noticed he was empty-handed.

"Oh bloody hell. Sorry, I got distracted. I went to get us a beer and got talking to this lovely couple who asked me to try this local tea."

"What type of tea?"

"I'm not sure. It was delicious, so I had two."

Max's removed his glasses - his pupils were bigger than the coconut glasses he was wearing.

Whatever was in that tea was definitely not PG tips. I quickly put his glasses back on him and pulled him aside so nobody could hear us.

"How many fingers am I holding up?" I grabbed him by the arm and held up my hand.

"Three, and they're not your fingers, they're your toes. Do you think I'm drunk or something?" Max giggled.

He was dancing all over the place like an acid-crazed Duracell bunny, then darted into the sea fully clothed. I chased after him shouting at the shoreline, begging for him to come back.

I went to find Maddie to see what we should do.

"It's only mushroom tea. Very diluted. He'll be fine." Daniel didn't seem too worried. "Seriously, it will wear off. Just be normal with him. Don't make him paranoid."

"Chill out, girl. We're at a beach party in Hawaii. Stop worrying and just enjoy it," Maddie said, not removing her gaze once from her new love interest's eyes.

Thankfully, Max he had dragged himself out the water and was laying on the floor staring up at the stars. I lay next to him.

"I often wonder what's up there, don't you?" Max asked, putting his arm around me. "Did you know there are more stars up in the sky than there are grains of sand on this beach?"

Suddenly the music stopped and we heard sirens and dogs in the distance. I sat up to see what the commotion was.

"It's the cops!" Daniel and Maddie ran over to us. "We've gotta get out of here."

"Please vacate this beach," a police voice said over a microphone. "This is an illegal gathering."

"Shit, make a run for it, mate," Daniel urged.

"We can't leave Pete." I panicked as the police were getting closer.

I spotted him under a tree still chatting up the girl.

"Sorry, we've got to go." I rudely interrupted Pete and dragged him with me. "The police are here. They're gonna catch us."

"You've got my card. Call me!" Pete shouted as we headed back to the dock.

We piled in the tiny boat back over to the surf shack and jumped in Daniel's car. My heart was jumping out my chest as I looked back for the police search light.

"We've lost them!" Daniel said whilst revving the engine.

"Let's go!" I pleaded as we pulled out the car park. "I cannot get arrested on this cruise top of everything else."

"Chill out, girl. We're grand now," Maddie reassured me.

"Why did we leave so early? We were only just getting started." Max was disappointed and totally oblivious to what had just gone down.

After what felt like hours, we got back to the port. Hiding our faces and avoiding all eye contact with the general public, we queued up to get on the ship. Thankfully, there were no guests about.

"Heavy night was it?" the same security guard we pissed off in Acapulco asked.

"No, not really, just been for an early morning stroll," I replied very unconvincingly.

"In the clothes you went out in last night?" The guard asked. "This tells me you lot left yesterday evening." He pointed to the clocking in system. I giggled nervously and patted him on the shoulder.

We crept back to our rooms for a couple hour's worth of sleep, praying Max's mushrooms had worn off in time for work.

CHAPTER FOURTEEN
Fish Guts/Hot Dates

DATE:15 FEBRUARY 1998

DAY AT SEA (CROSSING THE INTERNATIONAL DATELINE)

ENROUTE TO: PORT DENERAU, FIJI

CRUISING THE SOUTH PACIFIC

"Bianca, don't forget you're taking part in the crossing the line today. Be there at 3.00pm," Pete reminded me as soon as he walked in the office. "Wear something old that you don't mind getting wet and dirty."

"I don't want to! I've just washed my hair," I protested, sulking in my chair with my arms folded.

I'd learnt that morning from Max that every world voyage, when a ship crosses the equator to travel south on the globe, there is a special ceremony that takes place. Ours took place between leaving Hawaii and sailing to Fiji.

For those crew members who'd never crossed the equator line before, it was compulsory to take part in the initiation, especially if you were part of the entertainment team. I had no escape from it.

The ceremony involved some 'Mermaids' (played by the beautiful dancers obviously), a 'King Neptune' look-a-like, and lots of crossing the line 'virgins' i.e., me, being covered in gunge and then thrown into the pool. Played out in front of all the passengers and crew. It really didn't sound like my cup of tea.

"Once it's done, it's done. We all had to do it in our first contract." Pete winked at me, trying to soften up my sulk.

It didn't really matter how much I protested, I had to do it on Cynthia's orders. Even some of the guests wanted to watch the 'weather girl' take part.

"You'll never be a shellback if you don't do it!" Pete mocked. "New sailors are all tadpoles until you take the plunge, then you get anointed into a shellback," Pete explained. "When we cross the equator, we're crossing the international date line, so we actually gain a day going over. So we're going to have two days of the same day."

I was baffled. I couldn't quite get my head around it.

"So I have to live this day twice?" I was wondering what the gunge would be made up of.

"On the way down we gain a day, so tomorrow is today's groundhog day, and on the way back we lose a day," Pete tried to explain, but I was utterly lost. I would just have to experience it for myself.

Pete and Max left the office for lunch, so I was alone to get on with my work. I wanted to get finished early so I could go and sunbathe on the crew deck. We were halfway around the world already and I was still as white as a sheet. I needed a bit of tanning time on such a beautiful sunny day.

There was a knock on the door and I could not believe who walked in: it was Ravioli holding some kind of black box.

"Can I help you?" I stood up and ran to the door as quickly as I could.

"I hope you don't mind me to come to your office." He was whispering and looking rather shifty. "I wanted to know when I would see you again?"

"Look I told you, I can't see you again. I have a boyfriend and you used to go out with my friend." I was terrified of Maddie coming in and this little debacle becoming common knowledge.

"Then I have to watch you on the TV and wait you change your mind." He pointed to the hard drive in his hand.

"What do you mean?" I was confused.

"My friend's the camera guy and I ask him for your weather reports so I get to see you when I want." He smiled and did his puppy dog eye thing again.

It took me a moment to process what he had just told me. The whole situation made me very uncomfortable.

"I'm sorry, but if you don't leave me alone I'll tell Maddie." I put my hand on my hip, very matter of fact.

"How did you know?" His voice trailed off as the penny dropped.

"Well, I do know. So please, leave me alone and take me off that bloody hard drive. I'll go to the captain and tell him you're stalking me." I was very stern at this point.

It looked like this threat got through to him and he scarpered down the corridor. I'd only met him for one drink once, the weirdo. Imagine if I had pet rabbits? They'd have been boiled to death by now.

I was dying to tell Max what happened, but obviously I couldn't tell anybody. I decided if the sleazebag came back again after my threat of the captain, then I'd have to confess and get help.

I threw on my bikini, grabbed a towel, and raced up to the crew deck. Max was already there, sprawled out on one of the loungers with his blue and white striped towel perfectly matching his swim shorts, so colour co-ordinated and immaculate. He put me to shame.

"Sorry I'm late. Busy morning." I put my towel on the bed next to him. "How the hell are you feeling today Mr.?"

"The last thing I remember is leaving you getting your face painted, then I woke up covered in sand with neon stripes all over my face this morning." Max had his head in his hands. "I don't know what happened. All I know is I feel like the walking dead today."

"Don't worry, you were fine," I reassured him. "You just drank a trippy tea and I looked after you. It could have been a lot worse."

"Please, can we never mention this again?" he asked. "I mean the tea part. I couldn't bear anyone to find out. I mean, I could lose my job if word gets out."

"What happened at the full moon party stays at the full moon party, I promise." We hugged, which I instantly regretted as I become very sticky and greasy from Max's tanning potion.

"Also, I have given up on Sergiy," he confessed. "I thought he was keen, but now I'm not so sure. There's only so many times I can be in the dance studio pretending I've lost my pager."

"Yes, put him on the back burner for now," I agreed.

"I'm sure I'm destined to meet a wealthy fashion designer who'll sweep me of my feet and take me to live in Milan to be his muse," Max said, very matter of factly.

"Definitely, I can see it now," I agreed. "Maximilian the Milan Muse."

I had only been lying there for five minutes and I was literally boiling in the heat. Max didn't flinch. He was perma-tanned anyway and oiled up like a treat. I splashed in the little pool to try and cool down.

"Bianca, where's your suncream? Your water?" Max asked as he spotted me flat in the pool, trying to cover my body with the 8 inches of water.

"I didn't bring any. I didn't have time," I shouted splashing the water over me. It wasn't helping me as the water was as hot as the sun.

"You can't come sunbathing under the equator that pale." Max walked over to me. "This is the hottest day of the voyage," He looked at me like I was mental.

Maybe it wasn't such a good idea. Earlier I had pre-warned the guests of the scorching weather report that day. I grabbed my things and went to get ready for the crossing the line ceremony.

The pool deck was packed. There were two decks looking down onto the main pool crowded with hundreds of passengers and crew. This was one event that crew were actually welcomed into the passenger area instead of being kept below decks.

'King Neptune' was stood next to his throne, arm in arm with his 'mermaids', and Cynthia shouting 'Order, Order'. It was very bizarre. This was another one of them magic mushroom moments, much like the Penguin episode.

I was placed into a 'crew tadpoles' queue and had to wait in line alongside the 'passenger tadpoles'. Everybody was there: the captain, deputy captain, hotel manager, engineers, nurses, doctors, everybody seemed to be taking it very seriously.

"They've been doing this since the 13th century, you know, on all kinds of ships. First the pirate ships, then on naval ships, cargo ships, passenger ships, even submarines," one of the guests told me whilst we were waiting in line.

"It used to be an old sailor test to see if new shipmates could handle long, rough times at sea. They've watered it down now, of course. Back in the old days you could have met your death."

Oh great. That didn't fill me with much enthusiasm.

"So what's King Neptune got to do with it?" I was confused.

"Neptune is the God of the sea, dear. He's asked to grant safe passage of the ship and her crew to go across the line."

It was making more sense now. Maybe I should have read up on my nautical history before embarking on a ship career. Well, I'd plenty of time to learn. I was a 'tadpole' after all.

The crew line was getting longer and from a mile off I spotted fit Davide looking right back at me. Great, I was about to be gunged and drowned in front of him, making me all the more alluring and appealing.

The ceremony finally began with Cynthia in a judge's wig and Pete dressed up as a heavily-bearded 'King Neptune'. Taking centre stage, reading dialogue from a script, Cynthia asked 'King Neptune' to grant us safe passage, then the music started and it was time for us to become 'shell backs'. I couldn't see what was going on in front, and the line was moving quite quickly with a very strong smell coming from the pool area. I was holding my nose when Davide appeared amongst the sea of faces and headed in my direction.

"I don't want to do this." He was waving the smell away with his hand.

"Me neither." My cheeks were burning up red.

"We can do it together then." He winked at me and I started feeling butterflies in my belly.

As we got closer to the front, it became more apparent what the gunge and the smell was - it was fish heads and fish guts mixed with rotten food and slime. I almost vomited in my own mouth. I wanted to run away, but I didn't want to bail out with Davide next to me.

„NEXT!"

Oh shit, it was my turn to be covered in fish and rotten food right next to the man of my dreams. Six of us crew 'tadpoles' were given a pair of goggles to protect our eyes, then we were instructed to sit on a bench the edge of the pool with our backs to the water.

Huge vats of gunge were poured over our heads. I wanted to scream, but kept my mouth closed for fear of swallowing any fish eye balls or brains, and kept my hands over my ears. I was kicking my legs in disgust as the gunge was rubbed in, then I was pushed backwards into the water. I came up for air and got a big mouthful of fish-flavoured pool water.

"Congratulations, you are now officially shell backs. Please vacate the pool area," Cynthia boomed over the microphone.

I pulled myself out to the pool, looking like I'd just been dragged out of a swamp, covered in fish with my skin turning a very dark shade of green. I grabbed a towel and rushed towards the crew stairs. I was making a run for it when I couldn't actually believe who was hot on my tail down the stairs. It was Officer Davide.

"Bianca, don't run away," he shouted after me.

I stopped on the staircase hiding my face behind the towel, I was so embarrassed I just wanted to get in the shower and bleach myself.

"Don't worry, I'm the same, too," he shouted down the stairs. "Now we're both official shell backs. Will you come for a day out with me in Fiji?"

"Just me and you?" I was gobsmacked.

"Yes, just us two? Is that ok?" He looked unsure.

I nodded.

"Ok, meet you on the gangway in Fiji at noon - I'll be waiting."

I nodded again. I couldn't say much I was in shock. I sort of floated back to my cabin in a smelly daze.

After all this time, Davide had finally asked me on a 'date'. If I'd have known it was that easy, I would have smothered myself in fish guts a long time ago.

CHAPTER FIFTEEN
Fun In Fiji

DATE:17 FEBRUARY 1998
PORT OF CALL: PORT DENERAU, FIJI
ARRIVAL: 7.00AM
ALL ABOARD: 5.00PM

Traditionally-dressed Fijian girls were dancing to the band on the welcome dock that morning. They were all drop dead gorgeous with long, dark, thick hair to die for. I was taking in the morning sun against the beautiful backdrop, trying not to think about my impending date with Davide. I was nervous!

I was waiting for our next VIP guests to arrive. Cynthia had given me a photo and info of each guest so I could pick them out on the busy pier when they arrived.

I was reading over the information. I was expecting two elderly ladies who were big time actresses back in the day. I'd never heard of either of them, but of course our guests would have. They used to act in all the big movies of yesteryear and one of them was an ex Bond girl.

A blacked-out limousine pulled up amongst the rows and rows of tourist excursion buses. Two ladies got out first, one incredibly tall and the other one around my height, dressed from head to toe in black - hats, fingerless gloves, sunglasses, everything. They were travelling with their husbands who were slightly behind them, struggling with all the mountains of designer luggage. They looked like they had just stepped out of the Hollywood Hills. I was very excited to meet them.

"Good Morning. I'm Bianca. It's a pleasure to welcome you on board 'Lady Anne' and escort you to your rooms on behalf of Cynthia La Plante." I held my hand out to greet them both.

The smaller lady smiled and shook my hand. The taller more stern-faced lady just looked me up and down. She had a black veil hanging from her floppy black hat. She definitely didn't want to be recognised.

"Can you get a bell boy? My husband needs help with our bags." The shorter lady pointed over to her poor out of breath husband.

"Right away." I paged the bell boy to come and assist.

"Pleased to meet you. I'm Eva and my husband is Miles and this is Tina and her husband George." The tall lady still said nothing with her lips pursed together.

George (the tall lady's husband) appeared to be around half of his wife's age. He was very handsome and so charming that he kissed my hand instead of shaking it. He was much more friendly than his wife.

"If you could please follow me to your penthouse suites, we are going to take a little shortcut." I beckoned them on to the gangway and passed through security whilst trying to work out the least strenuous way to get these people to their rooms.

"Follow me please," I said enthusiastically. I was determined to get the tall lady to smile.

After about three flights of stairs and complaints of aching joints and Eva's husband's pacemaker possibly giving in, we took the elevator to their penthouse suites.

There I was, little Bianca Drake, in an elevator making small talk with these big time Hollywood actresses from the glamour era. You couldn't make this up.

I introduced them to Bentley their butler, Dr. Riley's butler from before.

"When will we know when our talks are, dear?" Eva asked.

"Tonight we'll have a meeting about your schedule. Please call me if you need anything." I trotted off down the corridor.

"Excuse me, Bianca. Before you go, Tina would like a word." George waved me back to their room.

"I don't like it." I wondered what Tina didn't like. Her hat and veil were now removed. I noticed that her face didn't move much when she spoke.

"This isn't what I requested. I asked for a port side suite and this is clearly starboard." She pulled a piece of paper out of her black designer bag.

"I'm very sorry, madame. I'll check with your butler." I was a little taken aback. What difference did it make? The ocean looks the same from every angle when you're crossing water.

I could only imagine what her house back in LA was like if this suite was not good enough. She must have lived in a bloody castle. I went to speak to the butler, who quickly arranged for Tina and her luggage to be moved to the exact same room but on the port side.

"We'll be moving all your luggage to an identical room adjacent to this one. Is there anything else I can help you with?" I asked, hoping the answer was no.

"Yes, I want white lilies every morning before sunrise. I awake at 6.30am, so shall expect them in the living room area before then."

I nodded and took out my notepad.

"A jar of freshly picked rose petals every evening by 5.00pm for my evening bathing, and fresh lavender by 10.00pm each night for my pillow to help me to sleep."

I didn't know where we were supposed to get this lavender from when we were sailing the oceans. I prayed the on board florist was well stocked.

"Actually, just take a photocopy of this list and bring it back to me."

She passed me a three page list.

"Of course. Is there anything else I can do?" I asked.

"Is it you who arranges our talks?" She raised her eyebrows.

I nodded meekly.

"Then I need to speak to both the sound and lighting engineers. It needs to be vision and pitch perfect. When I'm talking onstage, I require a head set with a pointer and then of course my dressing room requests."

"We'll be meeting later to discuss your talks." I'd never encountered anyone this demanding. This woman made Cynthia look like Mother Teresa.

"Thank you, Bianca. You're a Gem." George patted me on the shoulder.

He was so laid back compared to his wife. I hoped she would loosen up a bit when the cruise got underway.

"Nice to meet you. Enjoy your voyage." I made a sharp exit back down to work. I had to finish the daily newsletter, do the weather report, then get ready for my hot date!

"Enjoy your day in fabulous Fiji, ladies and gentlemen," I told the camera. "Myself and Max are fulfilling a lifelong dream and going fire walking over hot coals today with a local tribe on one of the outer islands. As you can imagine, I'm nervous, but we're taking the opportunity to fully submerge in local culture. I'll let you know how I get on tomorrow." I had to stop myself from giggling. "I hope you have a lovely day. As always, please take water with you for rehydration and don't forget your sunscreen. It is going to be a scorcher today, ladies & gentlemen." I was such a pro now with the whole weather thing. Who knew?

I finished the filming and quickly removed my microphone. I was done with work for the afternoon. I was laughing to myself, imagining myself and Max attempting to walk across hot coals. There was no way anyone was going to fall for that story.

"Enjoy your day in fabulous Fiji, ladies and gentlemen," I told the camera. "Myself and Max are fulfilling a lifelong dream and going fire walking over hot coals today with a local tribe on one of the outer islands. As you can imagine, I'm nervous, but we're taking the opportunity to fully submerge in local culture. I'll let you know how I get on tomorrow." I had to stop myself from giggling. "I hope you have a lovely day. As always, please take water with you for rehydration and don't forget your sunscreen. It is going to be a scorcher today, ladies & gentlemen." I was such a pro now with the whole weather thing. Who knew?

I finished the filming and quickly removed my microphone. I was done with work for the afternoon. I was laughing to myself, imagining myself and Max attempting to walk across hot coals. There was no way anyone was going to fall for that story.

"Do I go laid back beach babe or smart casual?" I was in front of the cabin mirror trying to get my date outfit right for the seventh time.

"You're in Fiji, mate. Throw a bikini on and a vest over. Jeez, you British girls are so fussy." Lisa poked her head from under her bed covers looking rough as hell. I'd heard her crawl back from the crew bar about 4.00am that morning.

I was so glad I was fresh for the day. I mean, today was the day. I was going on a proper grown up date with the mystery man I'd fancied for weeks.

I took Lisa's advice and finally decided to wear a bikini with a lace throw over dress, sandals and my straw hat. I was trying to control the butterflies in my stomach when there was a knock on my cabin door.

"I came to wish you the best of luck. Of course Davide should be taking me on a date instead, but I don't think I'm his type." Max laughed. "He seems like a nice guy. Very shy though, so it's probably best that you do the talking and bring him out of his shell - IF he speaks any English," he teased.

"I still can't place his accent and I don't even know where he's from." I panicked.

"Well, let's hope he can understand yours." Max laughed.

Max offered to walk me down to the gangway to help me relax as I was so nervous.

"Bianca, he's only a boy, albeit a very good-looking one. Just a shame it's too early for a drink to calm your nerves."

We got to the gangway and there he was, waiting for me, leaning against the wall with a little backpack on looking as gorgeous as ever.

"Have fun, you two," Max shouted as he continued back to work.

"Glad you could make it." There was a split second where we were going to greet each other with an awkward kiss on the cheek, then decided to go for a much more formal handshake.

"Thanks for inviting me," I beamed. "I've never been to Fiji before, have you?"

"You know, I have been at sea for a while, but never outside of European waters, so all this is a first for me, too. First world cruise, actually."

I could detect a Mediterranean accent, It was so sexy.

We exited the gangway past the Fijian girls who were still dancing on the quay side.

There was a very long silence until we got out the pier. I was waiting for him to tell me where we were going, so I began to do the talking.

"So where are we going?" I asked.

He pulled a little map out of his backpack and showed me that there was a little bus you could take that did a circular of all the nearby hotels. He figured we would hop on and off until we found the nicest place to have lunch in. So he had this planned all in advance. He was getting cuter by the minute.

We jumped on an old rickety open air bus with a thatched roof and sat at the back making small talk as we drove up to the resorts.

There were dozens of hotels against the backdrop of the blue sea and palm trees blowing in the wind. Davide was telling me snippets of information about the port we were in. He knew a lot considering he had never been before. I was surprised to learn that Fiji is one of 322 islands. I thought it was one big one. I definitely needed to go back to geography lessons.

"How do you know all this information?" I asked.

"When you are in my job, you have to, plus all the navigational information. I find it incredibly interesting, one of the more exciting parts of the job."

Wow, his English was a LOT better than I expected. It was probably better than mine. What on earth was I worrying for?

We decided to have lunch at one of the posher hotels we saw on the bus ride. This one had the restaurant actually on the beachside with the tables in the sand. It looked amazing. 'Lady Anne' was in the same bay. We could see it a bit further out.

"Table for two, please," Davide asked the impeccably dressed waitress. "Can we have the one under the canopy?" He chose the nicest table on the beach, covered by a canopy draped in white nets. I shuddered to think how much this lunch was going to cost.

We had a beautiful seafood lunch with nice white wine and chatted for hours. It wasn't awkward at all. He was very intelligent and had lots to talk about. He told me he was Spanish from Barcelona, he had been at sea for five years, and eventually he wanted to be captain. He wanted to know all about me, but not in an interrogative way like Officer James. He wanted to know how I really hurt my leg, and why I was in such a mess the night he saw me in Hamburg with snot all over my face. I was crying laughing, telling him a much diluted version of the stuffed tiger evening in NYC.

"Do you jet ski?" He pointed to a guy on the beach selling half hour rides. I'd never been on them before, but I didn't want him to know that. I was sure all the girls in Spain were jet skiers, and I didn't want to seem like some boring little English girl.

"Sure, not for a long time, though. Let's go," I bluffed.

Davide wouldn't let me pay a penny towards the lunch. I offered, but he seemed quite offended.

"Ladies don't pay where I come from," he explained. "It's not in my culture." Well, I couldn't argue with that, could I? We booked the jet ski and he passed me a lifejacket.

"Who's doing the driving?" the jet ski guy asked.

"He is. I'll get on the back." I smiled.

I wasn't so nervous for my first time on a jet ski. It must have been the white wine. I jumped on the back and held onto Davide, gripping his lifejacket for dear life as we sped off into the water. I was closing my eyes and grabbing on tightly as we went further and further out. After a minute or so I relaxed a little and opened my eyes to the bright blue sea. It was amazing, riding the waves with the wind in my hair. First time on a jet ski and I actually enjoyed it.

"Can we swap?" I shouted down David's ear.

"You wanna drive?" He slowed down. "Sure."

We came to a standstill then I climbed over and took the helm.

"You know what to do?" he asked.

I nodded and started the engine slowly.

"Let's go for a little drive." I pointed over to 'Lady Anne' basking in the blue waters not too far away. "Let's get a bit closer."

I drove (very well I might add) over to the ship, being careful to keep my distance and not get too close. It was so surreal looking up from the little jet ski to the huge ship. I felt tiny again, like on my first day at the Southampton docks.

A little old lady on the deck waved at me. I waved manically back. How cool was I driving round the ship on my jet ski? I did a lap of the ship as more and more people were waving at me from the guests on the open deck to the housekeepers below at the port holes. They were even waving at me from the restaurant. I felt so popular!

The weather girl jet skis around 'Lady Anne' in Fijian waters. I couldn't wait to tell my story for the TV show.

I was getting closer and going faster, showing off my newly acquired jet ski skills and waving like mad at the dozens of people now waving at me from every deck. Even the deck officers on the bridge were acknowledging me.

"I don't think you should get so close," Davide warned.

"Oh don't be silly. I want them to see it's me!"

I revved the engine to get closer in, then...

"Please back away from the vessel. You are in a safety breach," a voice over a loud speaker shouted.

"Please back away from the vessel you are in a safety breach!" The voice repeated.

I looked up to the bridge and could see an officer in white uniform bellowing into the public address system. Then the realisation hit me that all these very friendly people waving were not happy to see me, they were waving me to back off.

Oh dear!

I quickly turned the jet ski and sped back towards the beach, praying to god it wasn't Captain Cooper, or I was going to be in deep trouble.

"Do you think they knew it was us?" I asked as soon as we were safely out of sight of the ship.

"I'm not sure. I did tell you to not get so close." He shook his head.

"Can we swap again? I don't want to drive now."

I was too worried about what was going to happen when we got back on the ship. I spent the rest of the ride worrying about it.

"Don't worry, Bianca. They didn't see it was us." Davide tried to console me as we returned the jet ski and sat on the beach.

"If they did, then just blame me," he offered.

"Don't be silly. It was my fault getting carried away as usual." I shrugged.

I put it to the back of my mind and tried to enjoy the rest of our afternoon on my hot date. We lay on the beach for a while and went for a swim, and before long it was time to go back on board, so we caught the same bus back and headed to the cruise terminal.

We were waiting in line to embark the ship, chatting amongst ourselves, when I felt a tap on my shoulder.

"How was it then?" A middle-aged man in a rather noticeable toupee asked. "Did you do it?"

At first I thought he meant the jet ski ride, but then I saw him looking curiously at my feet.

"Did you burn them?" He pointed to my sandals. "I've always been fascinated with fire walking."

He looked at me intently, waiting for my reaction.

"It was amazing," I bluffed. "It was nowhere as painful as it looks. We had all the correct training from the tribesman, and you know what? It was a great stress reliever."

These words were pouring out of my mouth so easily, what was supposed to be a joke was now being taken rather seriously. I had to go along with it. I didn't want to disappoint the guy.

"You know, I wish I would've known that was a tour option to do today." The guy looked dismayed. "I double checked the tour brochure and it definitely wasn't in there."

"Oh, it wasn't. This was a very private tour. Max has a few friends out here who pointed us in the right direction," I replied very matter of fact.

"Oh, really, very interesting. How can I find Max?"

"He's gone to his cabin to rest and cool his feet down." I lowered my voice in case anyone else overheard the pack of lies coming out of my mouth.

"Let's just say his fire walk didn't go as smoothly as mine." The man headed over the gangway.

Davide looked on in bewilderment. "Don't ask." I whispered. "It was just a little joke."

"Bianca, were you talking about fire walking on the breakfast show this morning, by any chance?" Pete queried as I came into a very busy office.

"Nope, that's your expertise, isn't it?"

Pete went slightly pink as I reminded him of the fire eater girl in Honolulu.

"Well, the tours department have been inundated with calls asking where the fire walking tour takes place." He looked me straight in the eye. "The guests told the tour office the weather lady was talking about it this morning."

"Oh, yes I was. I was talking about the local culture of the tribesmen," I answered. "I was simply educating the viewers on the wonderful ports of call we visit."

I smiled angelically at him and continued with my work. I couldn't believe my little fairy story of my day in port had been taken as gospel, and that the guests wanted to take part. How funny!

"You missed all the drama today, Bianca." Max leaned over my desk, talking under his breath. "The captain was doing his nut because some lunatic was circling the ship really close on a jet ski. Everyone was waving them to back away and they just kept getting closer and closer."

I listened, wide-eyed, keeping as straight faced as possible whilst my heart was thumping through my chest.

In fact, all this fire walking talk had made me forget ALL about the jet ski drama from the afternoon. Davide and I had arrived back on board earlier with no questions asked, so I was hoping I had got away with it.

"They were going to send one of the security speedboats out to contain them. The bar staff said the girl looked like you, but I told them you were on a hot date with Mr. Wonderful. How was it, by the way?" he asked.

I hesitated as I wasn't sure if Max was trying to trick me into admitting it was actually me or he was asking a perfectly innocent question. I decided by his face he actually had no idea it was me and had even defended me in my absence - what a fabulous friend Max was.

"It was so nice. We had a lovely lunch and I really like him, Max," I admitted.

"Remember, Bianca, men on ships," he scolded. "Let's go for drinks later. We can go and watch the band in the jazz bar?"

That sounded like a great idea. I hadn't caught up with the musician guys for a couple of days, and I wanted to watch them play before they did the big crew bar night.

"One other thing, Bianca." Max stopped at the office door. "Why do the guests keep asking me how my feet are?"

CHAPTER SIXTEEN
Sky Tower Diving

DATE:21 JANUARY 1998
PORT OF CALL: AUCKLAND, NEW ZEALAND
ARRIVAL:8.00AM
ALL ABOARD:11.00PM

I was having this really vivid dream about my little dog Harry, who was back home with my nan. I dreamt he'd come to my cabin to visit me and sat on my knee whilst I was stroking him and he was sniffing me like he always did.

I was awoken from my slumber by the same panting noise and breath that I was so familiar with from my dog. I opened my eyes to come face to face with this huge dog pinning me down on my cabin bed, sniffing my every orifice. I looked to Lisa's bed to find that she had the same type of dog sniffing all over her, too. There were two!

I was too scared to say anything, so I just froze and held my breath. The two humungous sniffer dogs were on leads and being manhandled by a very official-looking lady in a customs uniform.

"Don't panic, girls. This is just routine procedure," the lady said, pulling the dogs off us. Then they were gone, on to the next cabin of sleeping crew members.

"What the hell just happened, Lisa?" I shrieked. I grabbed a baby wipe to clean my face.

"I should've warned you, mate. Officials here check every cabin on board for anything illegal coming into the country." She took a wipe from me and did the same. What a bloody wake up call.

I looked out of our tiny porthole. We were docked right in downtown Auckland with the famous sky tower just over the road. I was all set to have another girly day with Maddie when the cabin phone rang. It was Davide.

"I was wondering if you wanted to head out with me again today? Captain Cooper told me to visit the Sky Tower observation deck and see the views of Auckland from all the way up there.".

"Maddie's invited me for shopping." I tried to act as casual as I could. "On second thought, the Sky Tower sounds more fun." I was sure Maddie wouldn't mind me rearranging.

"Ok I will look forward to it." He hung up the phone.

Wow. He had already asked me for a second day out in port together. This did seem to be getting quite serious, by ship standards anyway.

"I bet this morning wasn't the first time Lisa has woken up next to a rough dog, was it?" Max joked as I got into work.

"I thought I was dreaming, then I had this Labrador sniffing me all over."

I opened my computer to an email from the head receptionist.

Dear Bianca,

We have had several noise complaints from guests regarding a drum rehearsal which took place from 2.00am this morning until 5.00am. These are the folk band guests travelling under the name of Skye Smith. Security were called and knocked on the cabin in question, but were ignored. Please can you ensure that your guests do not practise drumming between the hours of 10.00pm to 8.00am?

Thanks

Francine, Front Desk

Great. How was I going to get around that? I began to rack my brains trying to come up with somewhere they could practise late at night without disturbing neighbouring guests.

Then it came to me. The only place on board ship where we could play music late at night without ever receiving any noise complaints. The crew bar, of course!

That was it. I would arrange a night in the bar of live music. They could practise, we could listen, and I would be the most popular crew member on board 'Lady Anne' by bringing a live band to the crew bar.

I went to check with Cynthia, and to my amazement, she actually agreed with me (for once) that it was a good idea. All I had to do was make the posters to advertise around the ship and get them set up in the crew bar on the night. Easy peasy.

"Don't forget the 70s disco night." Max handed me a piece of paper. "There's the directions to the costume shop. If you see a pair of silver glitter platforms, pick them up and I'll give you the money."

Oh dear. I'd forgotten tonight was the Studio 54 themed party in the crew bar. I didn't have anything to wear. I already had my heart set on going as Debbie Harry, but I didn't have a wig.

My second date in port with Davide, and this time I couldn't wait. My nerves had faded fast and I was beginning to feel slightly more comfortable with him, despite his very distracting good looks.

In fact, he was quite the opposite to what I initially perceived him to be. I expected a conceited and arrogant guy, when he was actually very sweet and polite.

"So are we going to the top of the tower, then?" I asked as we walked into the pier together.

"Yes. Also, I have a surprise for you. It's something I have always wanted to do." Davide's voice trailed off. "One of my friends has two spare places, so we are going to base jump off instead." He looked very pleased with himself.

Frozen with terror, I tried to look really pleased. Was he for real? I would rather cut my own toes off with a hacksaw than jump off the side of a building.

"Me, too?" I gulped.

"Yes, he had two spare places, so I booked us on."

He pulled the tickets out of his pocket. "You told me about your love of high adrenalin sports, so I thought Bianca's gonna love this."

I smiled as convincingly as I could. This was all my own fault due to my slight over-exaggerations and the small language barrier between us. I was trying to make myself seem more interesting, just like I did on my resume. I got a little bit carried away when I told Davide how much I loved living on the edge and how I wanted to hot air balloon, base jump, shark dive, and climb Mount Everest.

"We can do this together. It will be fun." He put his arm around me to reassure me.

"Ok, yeah, why not?" I nodded, smiling through gritted teeth.

What was I talking about? I wasn't going to survive the jump anyhow. Either the rope would snap or I would die of fright.

Sweet Jesus! We crossed the road to the sky tower building. A lady gave me a leaflet at the entrance explaining there were two options at the sky tower: to base jump (on a wire) OR to sky walk.

The sky walk meant you walked around the outside deck in a harness rather than hurling yourself 192 metres from the sky.

I couldn't decide which sounded more appealing: slowly walking yourself to a near death or hurling yourself into one.

We took the elevator up to the base floor. My knees were knocking and I felt as though I was going to pass out. The welcome staff took our tickets and gave us the registration form along with the jump suit.

This was all happening too fast. I was just going along with it, but any minute I would be on the platform ready to jump and meet my maker.

Don't get me wrong, I liked to think of myself as a go-getter, but I wasn't someone who enjoyed free falling from sky scrapers with only a piece of rope to keep me alive.

"You will want a ladies small." An attendant passed me a red and yellow all-in-one suit covered in zips. I went to the changing room to put it on.

I wanted to just be honest with Davide and tell him this was my worst nightmare, but then I also wanted him to think of me as a daredevil carefree type creature. I decided to go with the latter, man up, and just do it. We met outside the changing rooms, both looking like multi-coloured space men.

"I am so excited to do this." Davide zipped up his jacket. "Ok, so, ladies first and I will meet you at the bottom?"

He pushed me to the entrance first. I edged out onto the silver platform and made my way over to the safety rope attendant with tiny slow baby steps.

I held on to the railings as tight as I could whilst the guy went through all the safety instructions. I was trying to focus on what he was saying, but when I looked down, I could see the tiny buildings and vast amounts of water hundreds of feet behind me. It all went very blurry and I felt incredibly dizzy.

"Now, turn around while I hook you up." The guy had the wire in his hand to attach to my safety suit.

"If you look to your left, that's where you smile for the camera as we capture your pre-jump."

I looked at the camera in sheer terror whilst the guy turned me to face him. What was I doing? Why was I prepared to jump off a building to impress a guy when I clearly had a bad case of vertigo?

"I can't do it," I gasped. "Please untie me. I can't do it." My head was spinning and I had lost all colour in my face. The attendant unhooked me and led me back indoors by the hand. I ran straight past Davide to the bathroom to vomit.

By the time I had thrown my guts up and had a bottle of water, Davide was on the edge of the platform ready to jump. He turned around blew me a kiss (!) then dived off the side. I got out of my safety suit and back in my clothes still feeling dizzy from the platform walk. He appeared twenty minutes later, looking very happy and high on life.

"That was one of the best experiences of my life." He smiled. "Bianca, why you did not tell me you were afraid of heights?" He looked confused. "I felt bad forcing you do this."

"I'm not!" I protested. "I am just not feeling too good today."

He laughed and shook his head. "I'm sure. I guess you prefer the shopping trips, right?"

We took a taxi to the shops to do some exploring. It was so pretty with the boutiques and cafes set in white wooden villas.

We had lunch in a little bistro, then strolled through a rose garden. There were rows and rows of roses of every colour that you could imagine, with the most beautiful aroma blowing in the breeze as we walked.

In the distance, I could see a bridal party having their photos taken. We sat on the grass for a while and watched the passers by.

"How are you enjoying the ship life?" Davide picked up a pale pink rose from the bush and passed it to me. I tried not to swoon.

"I love it. What other job can you say you wake up every morning in a different country?" I asked. "Oh, except if you are an air hostess on a flight," I corrected myself.

"You seem to always be busy walking around with your papers," Davide noted.

"I wish I had a bit more free time on the ship," I admitted.

"My boss is very nice, so I have a good time at work," Davide said. "I can see sometimes you look very stress." He stroked my cheek.

"Let's go and find some costumes for tonight." I quickly changed the subject. We headed off in search of the nearest fancy dress shop.

I got back to the office with a huge bag of glittery goodies.

"Look what I found, Max!"

We found a huge costume shop just ten minutes up the road from the ship, full of clothes and props from every decade. I collected as much gear as I could carry. Max's face lit up as he spotted the pair of silver flares I had bought him.

"Tonight is going to be a such fun." He danced around the office.

Cynthia popped her head in the door and called me to her office.

"Why aren't you in uniform?" she asked.

"I have just got back in from port. I was just going to..."

"Sit down." She cut me off. "I have a very important report I need you to record on file. This is of the highest confidentiality and does not go any further. This is a general report I have to carry out for our head office. I don't have time to type it up, so...." She handed me a dictaphone. "Please go to the privacy of your own cabin and type up on these report sheets, word for word what I have dictated." She passed me a folder full of official-looking papers.

I took everything with me straight down to my cabin and locked the door. The tape length was 110 minutes. This was going to be a long night. Now minute taker was also under my remit, and on top of that, I still had my newsletter to finish. Reluctantly, I kissed the crew party goodbye.

It took me hours to type the report from start to finish. I had to keep stopping and starting over and over again. At 11.00pm, I was finally finished. I left it on Cynthia's desk.

I still had my own work to finish, so went back to my desk and carried on typing away. I was really disappointed I couldn't make the party, especially after all the costume hunting I had done earlier that day.

Maddie came in the office looking for me.

"What are you doing here at this hour? Where's your costume?"

I told her I had a mammoth workload and I couldn't go anywhere until I had finished.

"That is awful. We have had this planned for ages." She looked very disappointed. "Try and come later on, even if it just for half an hour, love."

She left me alone in the quiet office. Everyone was done for the night and enjoying the party. About twenty minutes later I heard a little tap on the door. I was a bit nervous it was going to be Ravioli on the other side, so I was just about to climb in the stationary cupboard when Davide's face peeked around the door.

"I've been looking for you."

I didn't expect it to be him.

"I wanted to go to the party with you, but I have been calling and knocking to your cabin." He looked a bit lost.

"Give me half an hour and I will be done."

I couldn't disappoint everyone, could I? I had a full Abba outfit and platforms that needed to be rocked.

"Bianca! You made it." Max jumped all over me. "I've been looking for you everywhere."

"I'm sorry, I've been so busy." I pointed to my platforms and hot pants. "I just threw this together."

"You look fab," Max said, twirling me around.

The crew bar had been transformed into Studio 54. There were glitter and sequins everywhere, whilst the DJ was playing vinyls. Maddie was dressed as Cher, Max was Ziggy Stardust, Pete was Jim Morrison, Lisa was Donna Summer, everyone looked brilliant.

The party was in full swing and the playlist was epic. We were dancing to Sister Sledge and Earth Wind and Fire. Max was the star of the show, with his brilliant costume and very clever dance moves.

I got the feeling that Maddie was being a bit off with me. She kept cutting me short when I tried to tell her about my day.

"I can't believe you've gone off with him!" Maddie finally spat it out at the bar whilst we were waiting for our drinks. "Two port dates in a row, Fiji and New Zealand!"

"Don't be like that, Maddie. I've liked him since I arrived and he's really nice."

"Well I hope you won't need a shoulder to cry on when it all ends in tears, girl." She fumed. "Because that's all that happens with ship relationships!"

"That's not fair to say, Maddie," I argued. "They're not all like your ex!"

"How dare you throw that in my face!" She stormed off into the crowd.

On second thought, I probably shouldn't have brought up that sore subject. I hoped she didn't hate me.

"Is it true? We actually have the band playing for us in the crew bar? How did you pull that one off?" Max quickly changed the conversation.

"Well, you know me, Max. It's not what you know, it's who you know." I laughed.

After a few more dances and a couple of death stares from Maddie, I was ready to go home. There was an after party with the dancers, but I was too tired, so Davide offered to walk me back to my cabin.

"Would you like to accompany me to dinner tomorrow evening in the restaurant?"

Wow, he was keen. This was date number three already. I whole-heartedly agreed and gave him a peck on the cheek goodnight.

As I was taking my makeup off, I wondered how the hell had I pulled such a hottie? I still couldn't believe it. It was all going very well and he showed no warning signs of being a stalker/psycho/deadbeat.

I peeled myself out of my hot pants and boots and dived into bed. I was so tired I went out like a light.

My deep sleep came to an abrupt halt when the phone rang. It was still dark and Lisa still wasn't back.

"Bianca, we're about to go into a state of emergency. Get your lifejacket on. We have to get to our muster stations as soon as possible." Maddie sounded very worried.

My heart was pounding. This is what I had been dreading in the back of my mind since I joined.

"What? Why? How do you know?" I fumbled around for the clock.

"There is a fire in the funnel and the fire teams are trying to contain it. I have just had the call from the bridge to pre-warn us. I said I'd call you."

"Ok, I'll get my jacket on. I feel sick. What do we do?"

"Prepare ourselves for the worst. Don't leave for your station until the general emergency signal goes off."

"Ok. I'm scared!" I'd never been in a real emergency drill before. My heart was racing and my palms were all sweaty.

"Me, too, but we're a good team. I will call you back as soon as I hear anything." Maddie hung up the phone.

I ran to my wardrobe and put as much warm clothing on as I could. I put my woolly hat on, filled up a bottle of water from the fridge, and put my life-jacket on and sat there waiting with all kinds of terrifying situations running through my mind.

What if the fire couldn't be put out? Would we have to get in the lifeboats? Who would rescue us?

We were in the South Pacific Ocean at 3.00am. I felt like I was going to faint with anxiety and I was the one who was supposed to be calm and collected in the restaurant directing 800 passengers to safety on the microphone.

Twenty minutes passed and the alarm signals still hadn't sounded, which worried me even more. With no call back from Maddie, I prayed this was because they had managed to control the fire. Lisa staggered in from the party.

"What are you doing in your lifejacket, mate?" Lisa laughed.

"We're about to go into a state of emergency, Lisa! Didn't you know? You need to get your warm clothing and lifejacket on." I started pulling her lifejacket from the top of the wardrobe.

"Struthe mate, no, I didn't know. Who gave you the heads up?" Lisa was pulling her warm clothes out.

"The officers on the bridge warned Maddie. She rang me. I'm terrified."

Lisa stopped dead in her tracks. "Maddie told you? Shit, mate, I hate to tell you this, but she's pulling your leg. Maddie is in the dancer's cabin party. I have just been doing tequila shots with her." Lisa was shaking her head.

"Are you joking?" I felt like an absolute fool. If this was supposed to be some kind of practical joke, it was way out of line. "Ringing me at 3.00am, frightening the life out of me!" I was furious.

I rang the night watch officer up on the bridge just to be on the safe side, and he did not have a clue what I was talking about.

"Yeah, sorry, mate. She's supposed to be your friend. A jokes a joke, but that's totally out of taste." Lisa tutted.

I was fuming that Maddie would do that to me. I sat in my cabin in my full emergency rig out waiting for a life-threatening situation to occur, not believing for a minute that my friend would lie to me about such thing. I couldn't hold in my anger anymore, so I threw off my lifejacket and went down to the party to find the cow bag and give her a piece of my mind.

CHAPTER SEVENTEEN

Wellied En Route To Wellington

DATE:21 FEBRUARY 1998
DAY AT SEA
EN ROUTE TO: WELLINGTON, NEW ZEALAND
CRUISING THE SOUTH PACIFIC

As I opened my cabin door the next morning, I found a huge 'Sorry' banner taped to the opposite wall of our corridor with balloons all around the door. I guessed that was Maddie's totally over the top way of apologising for the night before. I wasn't ready to forgive and forget just yet. I'd only had two hours sleep and by the time I went down to the cabin party to have a word with her, she'd already left.

I received a call from reception asking me to go and pick up an invitation at the front desk. When I got there I was surprised to see the invitation was addressed to Miss Drake.

Dearest Bianca,
You are cordially invited to a cocktails and canapés soiree this evening held in your honour. Join us in celebrating

your weather reports and your hilarious stories. We think you are fantastic as the 'weather girl' and should be on national TV. We look forward to meeting you in person.
Best Wishes
F.O.B
At 5.00pm this evening in Cabin 6174 (aft)

What did F.O.B stand for? Who were these people? I was very intrigued. Did it mean that some guests liked me enough to want to throw a gathering? Just from my tiny clips on the breakfast show? I couldn't wait to meet them.

"It's all done and dusted. I've booked the hot air ballooning trip, Bianca," Max told me as I met him on the way to the office. "Up bright and early to meet at 6.00am tomorrow."

I was so excited. A hot air balloon ride had been on my bucket list forever, and we were about to do it for real the very next day, and over such a beautiful country as New Zealand. How lucky was that?

I told Max about the invitation for my first formal dinner in the restaurant that evening with Davide.

"Getting a bit serious with him, aren't you?" He mocked. "First there was alfresco dating, now the formal dinner. Make sure you look the part. They don't let just any riff raff in that restaurant, you know."

Maddie barged into the office looking for Pete and looking very hungover. I avoided all eye contact with her and continued working at the computer. I was still fuming.

She didn't try to speak to me, either. She'd come to check on a spa appointment for a guest. I think she got the message that I did not want to speak to her yet.

I'd far too much to do anyway. I had to start moving the drums down to the crew bar on a squeaky old trolley for the gig that night. I roped Max into helping me. We were halfway down the corridor pulling this giant drum kit when my dreaded buzzer went off. I searched frantically for the nearest phone.

"Where are you?" Cynthia demanded.

"I am just pulling the drum kit down to the crew bar with Max," I replied.

"Eve and Tina's talk starts in one hour. I trust you have everything well prepared for them?"

SHIT! I had forgotten to take the VIPs down to the stage for a sound check which was an hour ago. I daren't let Cynthia know, so I kept my cool.

"Yes, Cynthia all is in hand," I lied through my teeth.

I made my excuses to Max and went to collect the two ladies to take them down to the theatre. I took them through the back-stage entrance.

Luckily, I had stored all my crowd management tactics from the Dr. Christine fiasco in my head, so was running the waiting audience with military precision. The doors opened and the guests all neatly filed in to the theatre, taking their allocated seats like well-behaved children. I decided to allocate each person a seat ticket on the door, and then the overflow would be able to stand at the back. Surely, even Cynthia would be impressed at this?

The talk began and the ladies were showing old movie clips and photos from back in their hey day on the huge projector screen on stage; they were both drop dead gorgeous. Eve was a fiery red head and Tina a sexy blonde. It was mesmerising to watch them on stage talking about their careers from all those years ago. The crowd gave a standing ovation once the talk wrapped up. Even Cynthia looked pleased.

"I also got an invitation to the F.O.B party," Cynthia told me as we made our way out of the theatre. "Shall we walk there together?" she asked.

"Of course." I tried not to act surprised,

I wasn't used to being with her in a social situation. This was going to be very weird. We walked to the cabin together in silence before she finally warned me as we approached the door:

"Don't get carried away at this party. We have the department's reputation to uphold."

I didn't respond to her comment. She was putting a downer on it before we even got there. We rang the bell on the cabin door and waited in awkward silence.

"Welcome. Please come in." A short, middle aged man opened the door in a brightly coloured suit.

"Look everyone, our guest of honour has arrived." He grabbed my hand and led us past the bedroom onto the huge balcony overlooking the back deck. The room was quite crowded with a huge table in the middle covered in canapés, tiny desserts, and a big cake centre stage with the initials F.O.B. iced on to the top. The guests on the balcony clapped as the guy who answered the door introduced me.

"Please welcome little Miss Weather Girl, who makes us laugh every day on board." He shook my hand. "I'm John, party organiser, along with my partner Jeremy."

Jeremy looked about half of John's age and very cute. Jeremy explained that a large group of around twenty guys had all come on holiday for their annual cruise all the way to Australia.

"We watch the breakfast show every day," Jeremy explained. "When we first started watching the TV show, none of us could work out if you were for real or acting, because you're so funny."

"Then we began just getting up early to watch you," Nick continued.

They took me around the balcony and introduced me to their entire party, who were all very excited to see me. Cynthia hadn't said a word since we had arrived and she was watching me like a hawk.

"Welcome also to Cynthia La Plante." Everyone clapped again. Cynthia managed to crack a smile this time as everyone acknowledged her.

"Thank you very much for having us, gentlemen." She put on her professional stage voice. "Myself and Bianca have so much fun putting the TV show together every day."

That was the biggest lie I had ever heard come out of her mouth. The majority of the time she left the TV studio before I even got up there to do my bit.

"Oh yes, we have a blast." I smiled just as falsely as her. John filled up the champagne tower and offered everyone a glass.

"Not for me, thank you. I have to leave shortly." Cynthia declined. I was slightly dubious about having a drink in front of Cynthia, but then I decided to hell with it. This was my party and I would have a drink if I wanted to!

"Can we all have a picture with you one by one at the canapé stand?" Jeremy asked.

"Of course." I chuckled, still amused by the fuss I was creating. People asking for photographs with me was so ridiculous. They all formed an orderly queue to get a shot with me. By this point, Cynthia definitely didn't look too happy that the focus was on me. She made her excuses and left the party. I felt more relaxed once Cynthia had left and began to come out of my shell a bit more.

"I loved the glitzy invitation you sent me today," I told Jeremy. "Can I ask what F.O.B stands for? I'm intrigued."

"Didn't you notice our badges?" He looked very disappointed.

I wasn't the most observant person, but then I noticed they all had round badges on the left breast of their jackets. Philip took his off and passed it to me for closer inspection. It was hand painted all the colours of the rainbow with a little sketch of a girl pointing at a map with the initials F.O.B running under the image.

"See, it's you! We made badges for our fan club and obviously F.O.B stands for Fans Of Bianca." Jeremy was very pleased with himself. "I designed these badges myself."

"This is so sweet of you all. I can't believe you have done all this just for me. I am so grateful." I felt a little overwhelmed. Today F.O.B., next, the 'Today Show', then maybe even a slot on 'Loose Women'.

They asked me about my weather girl stories and if any of them were actually true. I told them they were mostly true, but some were slightly exaggerated. They especially loved the walking across hot coals in Fiji story. When I told them about my hot air balloon trip in Wellington, they were very impressed.

"Why don't you do your weather report live from the hot air balloon?" One of the guests piped up.

"What an amazing idea. I'll check with Cynthia." We all fell about laughing. "Let's see if the camera can fit in the basket, too."

The sun began to set over the horizon against a sky of a beautiful burnt orange colour. We had the perfect sunset for a lovely evening. I felt like I'd known these guys a long time. They were so friendly and super excited to have me there. We proposed a toast and they invited me to come and stay with them in the West Village in New York whenever I was in town (an offer I was definitely going to take them up on).

I ate one last piece of chocolate cake and arranged to meet up with them again. I had to leave, the time had crept up and my dinner date was in thirty minutes.

I raced up the stairs to the restaurant entrance in a full length dress and five inch heels. Davide turned around and spotted me and smiled. My heart melted. He looked drop dead gorgeous in his black and white formal officer uniform.

"I thought you had forgot me," he said as he put his arm out for me to link him. "You look very beautiful."

He would have run a mile if he had seen the state of me ten minutes before. Thank god I didn't still have red lipstick smeared all over my teeth. The restaurant was jam-packed of glamorous ladies in their formal gowns and gentlemen in their tuxedos with dickie bows. It was a very elegant affair with a harpist playing in the foyer.

In the centre, there was a huge dining table with the captain at the head of it chatting and making jokes with everyone. The only time I had ever been in there was when it was empty and we were doing our safety drills. It felt so strange to be on the other side, going for dinner with a handsome man on my arm all dressed up. I actually felt like a guest for once.

We were escorted to our table on the upper level. Davide pulled my chair out for me, but I misjudged it. I missed and ended up on the floor. He looked horrified and picked me up, apologising profusely with all the surrounding tables laughing. I quickly jumped up and pretended it didn't happen.

"Are you ok, Bianca?"

"Yes, I'm fine. Don't worry." I shrugged it off.

We ordered our food and a huge jug of water. Davide kindly surprised me with a bottle of champagne. I didn't want him to know I had already had a few, so I willingly obliged in having a toast.

I told him about my 'Fans Of Bianca' experience as we drank and ate lobster. Then told me stories of what it was like back home in Spain, and how it was a toss up of going into the military like his father or joining the ships, when we were rudely interrupted by the dulcet tones of Cynthia.

"Good evening, ladies and gentlemen."

I couldn't mistake that raspy booming voice. I looked over the balcony to the lower level, and there she was, microphone in hand, dressed like the sugar plum fairy.

"Must she be everywhere I go?" I muttered to myself.

Then I remembered it was the night of the Chef's Parade. Cynthia presents to the guests the chefs that have been preparing all the meals for the cruise.

The music came on and the chefs walked around the restaurant whilst all the guests waved their napkins around their heads, so I followed suit.

That dinner was the best food I had eaten since I joined the ship. We were absolutely stuffed, but still ordered the dessert, coffee and petit four. I thought my dress was going to burst.

"Bianca, you have something on your face." Davide leant over to remove something from my cheek.

"What is it?" I was blushing.

"I think it is a piece of mashed potato from the main course." He wiped the mess into his napkin.

Due to the copious amounts of alcohol, I didn't care. I had eaten my own body weight in food in front of this guy, and managed to smear mash all over my face, and I was totally fine with it.

I wanted to go dancing up to the nightclub to meet my 'fans', but Davide was sensible enough not to let me, and walked me back to my cabin.

"I had a nice night." He kissed me on the cheek. "You are funny, Bianca. You're a very pretty clown."

Pretty clown? I didn't know whether I should take that as a compliment or brush it off as a miscommunication. Either way, I had never been called a pretty clown before. I loved the language barriers, it was so very entertaining.

Davide walked off up the corridor, waving me goodnight and blowing me kisses in the distance.

I wondered how long would it be till he actually kissed me instead of a hen peck on the head or cheek? He was very old-fashioned, and that made me like him even more.

CHAPTER EIGHTEEN

D Day

DATE:22 FEBRUARY 1998
PORT OF CALL: WELLINGTON, NEW ZEALAND
ARRIVAL: 5.30AM
ALL ABOARD: 7.00PM

It was 6.00am, on a very clear and crisp morning with the sun just about to rise over Wellington. In one hour's time, I was set to leave the ship for a morning of hot air ballooning with Max!

Before we set off on our little trip, it was time for Eva and Tina to disembark the ship.

"Thank you for all your help on this cruise, Bianca. You have been wonderful." Eva kissed me on the cheek. "Anytime you are in Los Angeles, drop me an email. It would be really lovely to see you again."

I escorted them to the waiting limousines and waved them off as they drove into the distance. I could just picture them flying first class back to a plush mansion in the Hollywood Hills. I would definitely write to them so I could go for a visit.

It was time for me to get ready for my excursion, in the hot air balloon! This was the kind of thing people could only dream about, and there I was, doing this whilst sailing around the world. I felt so lucky.

I was getting changed in my cabin when the phone rang. Little did I know my day was about to come crashing down around me.

"We can't go this morning, Bianca. Cynthia is on the warpath." It was Max. "There's a crew drill this afternoon, so she decided last minute that she should keep the team on board this morning for a safety training session." I was dumbfounded.

"What about our trip? We've paid." I was starting to get upset. "We've paid the deposit."

"We can't go. She won't let any of our team off the ship until we pass the safety questions," Max re-iterated. "I tried to reason with her already. She's well aware of how much we have paid."

"Can we re-arrange for this afternoon then?" I asked hopefully.

"I already rang and asked them. They only do morning tours."

I was absolutely devastated. We could have done the training on a day at sea. Why do it on the port day that all the crew had been looking forward to?

"I've prepared you all a safety exam based upon the 'Safety At Sea' Handbook." Cynthia slammed the papers down in front of the huge projector screen. "After the training, there'll be a revision session, then we shall take the test. Results should be 98% and over. There is no room for error where safety is concerned."

I couldn't concentrate on her safety session, there were so many of us in that training room. Everybody in that room looked as upset and annoyed as I did. It had taken us two months to sail there and none of us could go ashore.

"It's only until midday," Max whispered over my shoulder. "We will go and do some sightseeing," he offered, trying to make the best out of a bad situation.

Two hours, a revision session, and an exam later, and it was finally midday. Everyone gave in their papers and made a mad rush for the door.

"Bianca, were you planning on going out this afternoon?" Cynthia shouted after me as I was half running to escape. I stopped dead in my tracks, looking at Max in despair.

"Yes, I was. I had hoped to especially after having to cancel the trip this morning." I walked over to see what she had in mind for me. Max hurried out the door, leaving Cynthia and I alone.

"There'll be plenty of ports to do tours in. Besides, have you heard how dangerous those balloons can be?" She completely dismissed my disappointment and gave me her orders for the day.

"I have a big administrative task that needs doing and our next VIP guest arrives at 2.00pm, then the emergency drill at 4.00pm, so I suggest you make plans with Max some other time." She straightened her jacket and looked me straight in the eye. "Bianca, you are here to work. This is not a holiday."

I could feel my eyes welling up, but I fought the tears back. I did not want to show that she had finally got to me.

My important admin task that couldn't wait was printing off letters then delivering them to all the cabins on board. That would take all afternoon. I took this job to see the world, and there I was in one of the most farthest away countries you could possibly think of, and I couldn't set foot off the ship. I was so fed up. The only thing that kept me going was the thought of seeing Davide again that night.

I had just stuffed the last envelope and was about to begin delivering them, when Cynthia asked to see the letters before they went out, so I took a couple of examples into her office. She snatched them from me and inspected them with great concentration, both with and without her reading glasses.

"These names and cabin numbers are not centre aligned on the envelope." She threw them down onto her desk.

"Are you sure?" I picked one up to double-check.

"Absolutely, they are 0.5 of a centimetre out. Please don't cut corners, Bianca. I need a reprint of all envelopes." She didn't even look up at me as she ushered me away with her left hand.

"Are you sure that's necessary? I have just stuffed them all and was about to do the cabin drop."

"The envelopes are sloppy. The letters are fine." She still didn't look up. "Please start again and let me see them before you post."

"I don't think I will have time to redo my work and meet the speaker at 2.00pm," I said, thinking out loud.

She thought for a moment. "I will ask the Art Gallery staff to meet him. They have to carry all his paintings on board anyway." She passed me an information pack on our new celebrity guest. "No time to waste, get back to it."

I nodded and went back to my office to take the letters out of the envelopes I had already stuffed to begin ALL over again.

The restaurant was packed at the safety drill with lots of new joining crew and guests. I was at the front in my orange lifejacket and yellow hat, guiding everybody to their seats.

Cynthia came in to do her usual checks around the muster station. When she asked me where I was up to with the letter delivery, I told her I hadn't had the chance to start that part yet, and she just scowled at me.

At that very moment I could see Davide coming through the restaurant entrance over Cynthia's shoulder.

He looked very relieved to see me. "Bianca, I have been trying to speak with you all day, but I keep missing you. I must tell you something."

Cynthia did not move and stood there with her hand on her hips listening in to our conversation.

"Excuse me for one minute," I said to Cynthia and then moved Davide under the staircase for some privacy.

"Make sure it's one minute. This is a safety drill, not an opportunity to socialise," Cynthia retorted.

Davide looked very worried. I'd never seen him without a smile on his face.

"I have to leave, Bianca. I have a flight tonight."

"What?" I stared at him in disbelief.

"My father has had a major seizure and has been sent to the hospital. I have to go on emergency leave, right now."

"Oh no. I'm so sorry. Is he going to be ok?"

"That is what we cannot tell up to now. I must get home to my mother. I am the eldest. It is my responsibility." He grabbed my hand.

"Of course, you must go home to see him." I swallowed the biggest lump in my throat.

Cynthia placed herself in my eye level and began tapping her watch. The drill hadn't even started, yet she was still getting irritated.

"I am sad," Davide continued. "I don't want to leave you so soon, but by the other side my dad is very sick."

"Don't worry about me. You need to get back to your family," I reassured him.

"Bianca! Can you please end your little meeting?" Cynthia came over to us. "This really is neither the time or the place."

For the second time that day I felt like I was going to burst into tears.

"I have to go. Please keep in touch."

"I won't forget you, Bianca. I'll try to see you again." We awkwardly shook hands as Cynthia watched over us.

I watched him walk out the door. He turned back and gave me a wave with the saddest face I have ever seen. I was finally getting to know him a little bit, and just like that, he was going to vanish. I felt sick.

"Please keep your boyfriends away from your work duties," Cynthia seethed.

"His father is sick, he's leaving the ship to go home, and he is NOT my boyfriend," I snapped back at her for the very first time.

"Not my problem, nor the hundreds of passengers whose safety you are responsible for." She marched out to the restaurant. I'd never felt so alone in such a busy room of people.

I quickly switched to my duties and did my safety speech over the microphone like the trained robot I had become, all the while inside my head I was replaying the short conversation that had just taken place underneath the stairs. I wanted to crawl up into a little ball and die.

After the drill had finished, I was beginning to feel a little light headed. I put it down to the fact that I hadn't eaten since breakfast. I decided to grab a quick bite to eat before I began my mammoth cabin drop. I went to the officer's mess and filled my plate with salad. No sooner had I sat down to take a mouthful when my buzzer bleeped. I jumped out of my seat to find the nearest telephone.

"Where are you?" Cynthia demanded.

"I'm just grabbing something to eat. I haven't had a chance to eat all day."

"Bianca, you have a thousand letters to deliver that I want done by this evening. There will be plenty of time to eat." She slammed the phone down. I stared down the phone in disbelief.

"I have to go. I'm too busy to eat," I shouted very loudly across the room to the waiting staff. I hadn't even had the chance to tell my friends about Davide leaving so suddenly.

I left the food on the table and ran back to the office as fast as I could. I stuffed the envelopes and delivered every single one in under two hours. I was exhausted, emotional, and very upset.

As soon as I got back to the privacy of my own cabin, I began to sob uncontrollably. I had finally cracked under the pressure. Cynthia had broken me down piece by piece, and I couldn't take it anymore.

I picked up the phone and arranged an immediate meeting with the Carl, the crew manager who saved me in Florida.

"What's happened, Bianca? You look awful." Carl welcomed me into his little office. I closed the door tightly behind me for fear of anyone eavesdropping.

"I need to resign. I can't take it anymore. I'm being mistreated on every level." I plonked myself down in the chair and burst out crying again.

"Who made you feel like this?" He passed me a box of tissues.

"Cynthia. I have struggled with her since day one. I have done everything she has ever asked me and never complained, but now she's finally got to me. I'm done. I give up." I put my head in my hands.

I was so relieved that I'd finally plucked up the courage to go and speak to someone who might actually be able to help me. Packing my bags and going home to people who loved me seemed so appealing, I didn't care if I had to pay my flight home from the other side of the world.

Carl asked me to go into detail about exactly what had been happening. I started from the beginning whilst he made notes for his report.

I'd been talking for fifteen minutes non-stop and when I retold him what had happened earlier that day, I began to get upset all over again.

"Please don't cry, love. I'm sorry you've had to go through all this."

"Have you been getting the correct amount of sleep and eating properly?" He was making more notes.

"Not all the time. Sometimes I'm just too busy." I wiped the tears from my eyes. "There just aren't enough hours in the day."

"Have all these concerns been raised with Cynthia?"

"Yes, through Pete, but nothing gets done about it, then she just adds to my to do list to make my day even longer."

Carl finished typing his report and advised me that everything that was said was strictly confidential. He advised for me to go back to my cabin and rest whilst he addressed the situation with Cynthia. He told me to not do anything hasty until he had tried to resolve the situation.

I felt a bit better talking about it and prayed that something would be done about it.

I opened my cabin door to find an envelope stuck under the gap addressed to me. It was from Davide. In the midst of all the drama, I had temporarily forgotten that he had left me as well. I tore the envelope open and began to read it with my puffy, swollen eyes.

Dearest Bianca,

I'm sorry I had to leave so fast today. I came to say goodbye to your office again but your boss had sent around the ship. My flight leaves tonight at 8.00pm and I will think of you all the way home.

They think my father had a heart attack. I must be home to see him, I know you understand.

I'm not sure what's going to happen or when I'll see you again but I just want you to know that I'll miss you. I'll try my best to get back to the ship but I cannot even think about that until I know how my father's health is.

I hope to see you again.

Keep smiling for the weather reports.

Besos de Davide x

As if the day could get any worse, I had a gut feeling that was the last time I would see him. I felt so lonely, lost, and a million miles away from home. I rolled over and closed my eyes in an attempt to sleep the rest of the awful day away.

CHAPTER NINETEEN
Three's A Crowd

DATE:23 FEBRUARY 1998

DAY AT SEA

ENROUTE TO: MELBOURNE, AUSTRALIA

CRUISING THE TASMAN SEA

The first thought that pinged into my head the second I opened my eyes was that Davide had gone and I didn't know if I would ever see him again. Ship life sucked!

I had a phone call from Carl, asking how I was. I told him I felt a lot better after a lot of rest and asked if I should be worried about Cynthia at work this morning.

"About that, she was too busy to deal with me last night. I'm hoping to catch her sometime this afternoon when she's free," he told me. "She doesn't know you've been to see me, so don't worry, just carry on as normal, and if anything happens give me a call. I'm here if you need me."

The past few days had been a nightmare. My boss was a mega bitch, I had to cancel my ballooning trip of a lifetime, my potential future boyfriend had left me, and I hadn't eaten properly for days because I was too busy. I felt absolutely rotten.

I told Lisa everything that had happened and as I recounted the Davide part, that huge lump came back in my throat.

"You never know, mate, his dad may be fine and he could be back in a few weeks." Lisa sat on the end of my bed. "As for Cynthia, that's another story. She's been a lot more uptight lately."

Lisa tried to make me laugh by telling me about her awkward date the night before with one of the saxophone players.

"Mate, he found out about the ukulele player so he sacked me off." Lisa laughed. "Maybe I need to stop dating musicians, or maybe it's time to move on to the string quartet."

"You've a meeting at 11.00am in the new VIP's suite," Pete told me as I got into the office. "Can you ask him to only smoke in the designated areas? He's already been told, but if you can reiterate that to him that would be great."

I got the information pack out that Cynthia gave me to read over our new guest's details. His name was Giorgos Carlos, a very famous Greek/American painter. I was quite surprised to read that he was only forty two, which was very young for a 'Lady Anne' guest speaker. You usually had to be well over sixty five to talk on this ship.

"Can I come to his suite with you?" Maddie asked. "I've heard he's hot!" She put a cup of tea down on my desk for me.

"Can we be proper friends again now, Bianca?" She put out her little finger. "I'm so sorry."

I nodded and jumped out my seat to hug her. I was so ready to forgive and forget the ship drill joke, which seemed rather trivial compared to all the other shit I was going through.

"Sorry, you can't. I'll have to have him all to myself," I joked.

I knocked on Giorgio's door with my clipboard in hand, trying to look ever so professional. I'm not going to lie, a few more of the crew had told me he was very good looking, so I had done my hair and put a little bit of lipstick on, in the hope he might consider me as his next subject for his art. What girl wouldn't?

He opened the door in his white dressing gown, looking rather pissed off I had got him out of bed. He was very tall and tanned with big dark eyes and long black hair scraped on top of his head.

"I'm so sorry to disturb you. I'm Bianca, your personal assistant for the cruise. I am here to arrange your schedule." I put out my hand to greet him.

"Oh yes, I've been expecting you." He lit a cigarette as he looked me up and down. "Come on in." He spoke with an American drawl.

I didn't want to tell him he could only smoke on his balcony like I was told to. I'd only just met him. I didn't want him to dislike me from the get go. We went into the lounge area and sat on the cream leather couches. He finished his cigarette, then stood up and bent over to shake his hair out of the bun, then flipped it down his back just like a shampoo advert.

"Allow me to go and put some clothes on." He went into this bedroom to change.

Judging by the half empty Jack Daniels bottles and ashtrays strewn all around the room, he must have had a party the night before. He strolled back in with lots of black cross and skull necklaces across his chest and tight black skinny jeans with a white unbuttoned shirt over. He fit the bill of a rock star more than a painter.

"So, Bianca, tell me, where do you want me and when?" He sat on the couch next to me and leaned in close enough to me to smell the cigarettes and alcohol on his breath from the night before.

"I err, umm." I went bright red and pretended I was reading my clipboard. "What do you mean?"

"The talks? What have you got planned for my schedule?" He smiled cheekily.

Was this guy trying to hit on me this early in the morning?

I went through his schedules and talks that I'd prepared. He seemed pretty excited about the Art Gallery launch. As well as the talks, Giorgos was selling his paintings.

"Would you like a drink?" He cracked open a new bottle of Jack Daniels and got out two glasses.

"No, thank you. I can't drink on the job, and it's only 10.00am."

"What about later then?" he asked, filling his glass with ice.

How many times can you say you've been for a drink with a world famous painter? I decided to go, but take Max along with me so Giorgos wouldn't get the wrong idea. This was strictly professional. Besides, I couldn't stop thinking about Davide.

"Sure, I will meet you at 10.00pm in the piano lounge?" I suggested.

"I'll see you tonight." He winked at me as he showed me to the door.

It was afternoon time and I hadn't heard from Cynthia once. I started worrying that she'd finally had her meeting with Carl about me. At that very moment the phone rang.

"Did you meet Giorgos?" she shrilled.

"Yes, I did, at 10.00am,"

"Did you remind him of the designated smoking areas?"

"Yes," I lied.

"Can you go up to the buffet restaurant and remind him again? He's smoking a pipe in the dessert section and won't listen to any of the waiters up there." Cynthia sounded annoyed.

Why I was the one left to deal with this? I made my way up to the buffet to find Giorgos causing a slight commotion with the bar waiters. I could hear him telling them he was a VIP guest, therefore he could smoke where he wanted.

"Ah, here is my assistant." He waved me over to his table.

"You can go now. I'll deal with this," I told a very distressed-looking waitress.

"I'm sorry, Giorgos, you can only smoke outside on the deck in the designated areas." I put his pipe in the ashtray. "If you don't abide by the captain's standing orders, he has every right to throw you off at the next port."

"Really? Kicked off for smoking." He laughed. "Rules are meant to be broken, my dear."

"Not on this ship, I'm afraid." I decided to take another approach. "You do want to sell lots of paintings, don't you? I mean, lots of people are interested."

I could see his eyes lighting up at the thought of his art auction. He reluctantly agreed that he'd only smoke where he was allowed.

He asked where all the young guests were to hang out with. When I told him the average age range, he looked dismayed.

"Why don't you go up to the Spa and get a massage?" I was thinking of all the pretty young spa girls who would be swooning over him. With that in mind, he got up, Jack Daniels glass in hand, and made his way up to the Spa deck.

I bumped into Max on my way back to work.

"Bianca, you do realise Sydney is coming up and we need to finalise the seating plan for the world cruise dinner?" Max reminded me about the 800 strong table plan we needed to complete.

Every year, on every world cruise, 'Lady Anne' holds an extravagant dinner and dance on shore to mark our half way point of the cruise. It was going to take place in Sydney Town Hall and it was going to be a very grand affair. Max and I had lots of work to do!

"Wow, you look amazing." Giorgos stood up and kissed me on the cheek me as we took a table in the piano bar. He had his hair down, donning a very smart navy suit, looking very polished and handsome.

"Giorgos, allow me to introduce you to Max, my very good friend on board. I hope you don't mind him joining us."

They shook hands as I went over to the waiter to order some French martinis. I was still reeling over the Davide news. How could I not tell a fake like that? I needed another drink and FAST.

The martini went down very smoothly. I felt better straight away. Max and Giorgos were getting along like a house on fire. It turned out that one of Max's ex-boyfriends had one of Giorgos's paintings in his house, so he was well impressed. We chatted about Giorgos's work and how he was opening a gallery in New York. His stories were so interesting.

In my heart of hearts, I didn't really fancy him. He was very charming, but he just wasn't my type. This guy would've only been after one thing anyway, and that was not my style.

As a golden rule of Cynthia's, all crew must vacate the guest areas by 11.30pm, unless of course you are on duty. It was almost 11.25pm.

"Unfortunately, we need to go now Giorgos," I nodded at the clock behind him. "We have a crew curfew."

"Don't go now!" Giorgos said. "You must come back to my suite for some champagne." He called the waiter over.

I was about to protest when Max gave me the look and whispered, "We are going for a party with Giorgos Carlos. Don't even try to argue with me."

After no argument from me at all, we arranged to meet at Giorgos's room in ten minutes. He was ordering a take away bottle of champagne for us. Max and I had to sneak through the crew stairways to get to his suite. We would've been in big trouble if we were seen going into a guest room late at night.

"Bianca, we can't turn down an opportunity like this," Max reminded me as we made our way up the staircase. "What if he gifts me a painting or paints you?"

I didn't admit to him that I was hoping that very same thing earlier this morning.

We checked that security were not around, then knocked at his door and crept in his room on our tiptoes. The lights were dimmed, with soft flamenco music playing. There was an acoustic guitar leaning against the chaise longue. I should've guessed that Giorgos was a musician, too.

"Please, make yourselves at home." Giorgos took his shirt off and was sitting there in his suit pants. He lit a cigarette and sat on the couch.

"You know, smoking is reserved for the balconies," Max said. I nudged him to be quiet.

"What is it with that?" Giorgos asked. "I can't smoke in the bars, in the restaurants, or in my own suite. I hate formalities."

"It's just, you might set off the smoke alarm." I pointed to the ceiling.

He shook his head, picked up his guitar, and started to strum a few chords whilst tossing his hair back and forth. Max looked delighted at this renegade rockstar/painter figure we were hanging out with.

He showed us his art collection in the hallway.

We cracked open the champagne and toasted to selling lots of paintings. When Max popped to the toilet, Giorgos seized the opportunity to pull me close into him.

"You know, I think you will be my good luck charm on this journey," he whispered in my ear. "Maybe I should paint you."

I pulled away and made my excuses to go out onto the balcony for some fresh air. Well, he certainly wasn't backwards in coming forwards was he?

Giorgos carried on, showing off his guitar skills, then suddenly the song came to an abrupt end.

"Olé!" he shouted and threw the guitar down.

"Brilliant! The rock star who paints." Max clapped in appreciation.

"Thank you." He bowed and flipped his hair. "More champagne."

"Oh no, thanks. I must get to bed. I've an early start in the morning." I made my excuses.

"You can't go now," Giorgos said. "We're just getting warmed up."

To my and Max's amazement, Giorgos undid his pants zipper and dropped his trousers to the floor. He stood there in his black skintight underwear. Max and I looked at each other in disbelief.

"Rules are meant to be broken. Now come to the master suite."

"Excuse me?" I asked.

"Both of you. Let's make this a night to remember."

Shellshocked, Max and I just stood there open-mouthed. Giorgos had obviously forgotten that he still had his pants around his ankles. As he tried to make his way to the bedroom, his trousers got in the way. He tripped over them and THUD!

He face planted the floor and smacked his head on the hard wooden surface. He didn't move. He was face down. I sobered up instantly.

"What do we do?" I was panic-stricken. We weren't supposed to be in his room and now he was knocked unconscious with his pants round his ankles! This was not good.

Max kneeled down on the floor and gently tried to shake him, but it was no good. He was out cold. I grabbed the champagne bucket and emptied the ice all over him. Thankfully, he sprung back up from the floor and started coughing and spluttering. He looked rather dazed and confused, then quickly pulled his trousers up.

"My head hurts." He raised his hand to a small red mark on the left side of his forehead.

"It's just a bump." Max examined it. "We can call the nurse to check it?"

"That won't be necessary," Giorgos said, sitting up. "I've had too much to drink. I'll be fine."

Max and I helped him to his bed. I gave him more ice out the mini bar to keep the swelling down on his head.

Giorgos grabbed my hand and shook it manically. "Thank you for taking care of me. Let's keep this to ourselves, shall we?"

I nodded and smiled. I doubted he'd remember that he just offered myself and Max a three in a bed situation, anyway.

We crept out of the room and down back the crew staircase to my cabin. Lisa was staying out again for the night, so Max stayed in my cabin with me.

"Can you believe what has just happened?" Max burst out laughing once we were out of earshot and back in my room.

"Can you imagine Cynthia?" I gasped. "Giorgos Carlos found unconscious with his pants around his ankles. She'd have a fit and we'd be fired."

The mention of Cynthia's name reminded me that I had left a very important email unanswered.

"If I don't do it before the morning I will be in serious trouble," I explained to Max. **"I'll be back in five minutes. Listen for the door."**

Max climbed into Lisa's bed and yawned. I made my way up to the office, sent the email, and ran back downstairs. I knocked on the door gently. There was no answer. I knocked again a little louder, and then again, to no response. I was calling Max loudly under the gap in the door to try and wake him. I was so annoyed he wasn't answering. I was so tired, all I wanted to do was crawl into bed.

I sat on the staircase opposite my cabin door, waiting for Max to answer. I couldn't stop yawning, so I lay my head on the step, dozing off as I waited for him to open the door. This would unfold to be the biggest mistake of my sea career to date.

CHAPTER TWENTY
Sleeping On
The Staircase

DATE:24 FEBRUARY 1998 - 02.00AM

DAY AT SEA

ENROUTE TO: MELBOURNE, AUSTRALIA

CRUISING THE TASMAN SEA

"Where are you taking me?" I was bewildered to find myself strapped into a wheelchair. Who the hell were these people pushing me? They were all in white with hats on. Oh Jesus, it was the nurses. This was not good.

"We found her laying unconscious on staircase 13." I heard a guy dressed in full Hit Squad Hazmat gear telling the nurse.

Panic filled me as I quickly realised what a serious situation I was in. Reported by the Hit Squad, being pushed by the nurses, and heading straight for the medical centre.

"My cabin is that way," I said, a lot more panicked now that I had woken from my disorientated state.

"We're taking you to the clinic to check you out. We think you've hit your head when you fell down the stairs," answered the female nurse.

"But I didn't fall down the stairs." It all come back to me in an instant. I was locked out on the staircase and Max was in my room with the key. I didn't tell them that. I didn't want him to get in trouble with me.

"I was locked out. My room is just opposite," I pleaded.

The nurses ignored me and continued to push me in the opposite direction. Surely, they couldn't be doing all this just because they found me asleep on the staircase? My nerves were shattered and my knees began to tremble.

'Keep it together, Bianca,' I told myself. I wasn't doing anything wrong. I had a long day at work and was locked out of the cabin. I wanted to cry, but I kept myself together and acted as co-operative as possible.

The nurses unstrapped me from the wheelchair and I lifted myself onto the bed, then the crew doctor arrived to check me out. He did the usual checks and finally concluded that I had not hit my head, nor was I suffering from any kind of concussion.

He concurred with my story that I had indeed been sleeping on the staircase, even though it was a very odd place to take a nap. Right, that was that then. I was overcome with relief. Thank heavens the doctor backed me up.

"Can I go to bed now? I'm so sorry for all the trouble," I said.

"Bianca, we have procedures to follow, and I'm afraid this incident has to be logged and sent up to the captain," the senior nurse said very sternly. "We have to assume you've had too much to drink and have carelessly fallen asleep in a public area."

"But I wasn't doing anything wrong! I did have a few to drink, but that was earlier on. I'd just worked a very long day and I was locked out. Please, don't do this." I choked up as I realised this awful encounter could indeed cost me my job.

"You know the rules, Miss Drake. This is classed as gross misconduct."

I recalled Max's horror stories about being in the wrong place at the wrong time. I was in big trouble.

From nowhere, a wave of defiance and feeling of unjustness came over me. I wasn't doing anything wrong. I wasn't being aggressive, nor was I a danger to anyone else. I had simply fallen asleep on the staircase. The past ten weeks I'd been bullied, victimized, and worked to the ground, and nobody had done a thing to help me. Yet there I was, possibly going to lose my job, all because I got locked out (and maybe one too many Veuve Cliquout).

"Cynthia, can you come to the Medical Centre? One of your staff has been found in a situation," the senior nurse mumbled down the phone. This was quickly escalating from bad to worse.

"Why are you calling Cynthia?" I asked with my nerves trembling again.

"As she is your head of department, Miss Drake, and she must be present when I log the report."

That was all I needed.

Within minutes of the phone call, Cynthia appeared. Even though it was the middle of the night, she was wearing a full face of makeup and her hair looked as though she had just stepped out of a salon. Maybe she slept sitting up.

I heard once there was a helicopter evacuation on the ship and Cynthia was on the scene within three minutes from getting out of bed, looking as if she was about to present an award at the Oscars - now that was dedication.

"Oh Bianca, not you. I'd hoped it wasn't you." Cynthia seemed very dismayed and not anywhere near as angry as I had predicted. She looked slightly upset. I could detect a little bit of compassion in Cynthia's eyes for the first time. From the look on her face, I was going to be walking the plank, therefore before I did, I needed to state my case.

"This report will be sent up to the captain first thing in the morning," the nurse said. "You've not only put yourself in the firing line, but you've also used up the medical team's precious time and resources. If you're tired, you go to your cabin to get some rest, not sleep on a metal staircase. These are not the actions of a sober and sensible adult."

"I was locked out. Please don't do this. I work very hard." I couldn't control the tears rolling down my face. I repeated again what exactly happened with Cynthia present, as the nurse took more notes, stony-faced and silent.

By now, Cynthia's face had changed. That glimpse of humanity I had seen earlier was replaced with a look of disgust. The nurse left the room with the file and Cynthia shook her head.

"You've made your bed, now you must lie in it." She tutted. "Let me get you back to your cabin. I have a master key. Remember, this whole episode could have been avoided if you hadn't left the key there in the first place. Just what you were doing at your desk at that time in the morning I will never know." Cynthia's voice trailed off. We walked quietly from the clinic as Cynthia escorted me to my cabin.

I wanted to say 'Well actually, I'd forgotten to do something you asked me, and I was so afraid of you finding out that I hadn't done it, I ran to work in the middle of the night. If you didn't terrify me so much and wear me out physically and mentally, I would never have gone up to the office after hours and would never have got locked out. Drink or no drink.'

That was what I wanted to say, but what was the point? I had made my bed, as Cynthia said. She let me into my room and left me with one last icy stare just in case I hadn't melted from the previous ones.

I closed the door behind me and found Max still fast asleep on Lisa's bed with the cabin key on the dressing table next to him.

"Bianca, why did you take so long?" He sat up yawning, totally unaware I'd been gone for almost two hours.

"Oh Max, you're not going to believe what's happened to me." I went through the details. It sounded a lot worse said out loud.

"Bianca, I'll see Cynthia first thing and back up your story. I'll be your witness," he said as he wiped a tear from my eye. "What's a little nap here and there now anyway, hey?" He joked as he tried to make me smile. "That staircase is quite comfortable."

I couldn't laugh. My head hurt and now my heart hurt. How could I have been so silly to fall asleep there? I faced the prospect of losing my job and being sent home from Australia of all places, where I had always dreamed of going. I was literally two days away from getting there and I could well be on the first plane back home.

Fired from my job, friends I loved, and a ship I had come to feel at home on. England felt like such a long time ago. I didn't want to go back, and certainly not in those circumstances. What would my family say? They would be so disappointed.

I didn't sleep the whole night, going through all the possibilities and outcomes in my head of what tomorrow would bring.

CHAPTER TWENTY-ONE
The Morning After

DATE:25 FEBRUARY 1998

DAY AT SEA

ENROUTE TO: MELBOURNE, AUSTRALIA

CRUISING THE TASMAN SEA

In no time at all it was time for me to get ready for work and face the music.

'Pull yourself together Bianca, you reap what you sow' I kept telling myself.

I turned the shower on, pulled out my cosmetics bag, and plugged in my curling irons. I might've been getting fired, but I was sure as hell not going to look any less glamorous.

I could already feel the gossip spreading like wildfire around the ship without me even leaving my room. One thing I had learned is that gossip on ships is twenty times faster and over-exaggerated than in real life. I suppose that's to be expected when you have hundreds of human beings from all over the world living and working in a confined space.

I could just imagine it now, 'Did you hear about Bianca who does the paper? She fell from deck 12 all the way down to deck 1 and landed outside the medical centre with every bone broken in her body' or 'that girl who does the weather knocked herself out on a bottle of vodka' something along those lines.

Well, nobody knew the truth except me, and that was all that mattered. I took a deep breath and mentally prepared myself for the long day ahead. First thing first, I had to face up to my actions. I went directly to Cynthia's office and knocked gently.

"Come in." She didn't look up from her paperwork.

"Hello, Cynthia. I just wanted to say how sorry I am for last night," I said meekly.

She looked up as if surprised to see me. It made me wonder if I had already been dismissed.

"I didn't expect you for work today. I thought you may have been in your room, considering what happened."

"As I said, Cynthia, I wasn't THAT drunk, just exhausted. I hadn't eaten much, either," I replied, looking down to the floor.

"Well, for what it's worth, I'm glad you've pulled yourself together and are ready for the day ahead, whatever that day may bring. The show must go on, Bianca, the show must go on." She glared at me, then nodded for me to exit the office.

Outside, I breathed a huge sigh of relief. I was sure Cynthia would be telling me later I'd been fired, but for that day at least I had a daily newsletter to do, weather to report, and guests to look after. I entered the office and sat at my desk. Nobody looked up. Everyone was busy typing away. Maybe news didn't travel so fast after all.

I was thinking of what I could tell my family, and imagining the long aeroplane journey home. I could say that the hours of work were too much so I quit, or I had decided life at sea wasn't for me, but in my heart of hearts I couldn't lie to them.

What a let down I would be to all my family, a poor excuse of a drunken daughter. They'd say I was 'burning the candle at both ends'. I was about to go and get a phone card to call them when Max burst in the office.

"Bianca, can I talk to you about the guest from deck eight?" He was acting really shifty and trying to get me out the office.

We went outside where he beckoned me to the elevator without saying a word, so I stayed silent as the elevator sped up to the top decks.

"Ok, you need to sit down," Max said as we walked towards a bench on the open deck. "I've just been to see Cynthia to back up your story. I'm afraid it's not good news. You've to go up on the bridge to see the captain for a hearing."

"A hearing? Am I on trial? I feel like I've killed somebody, Max!" I wailed. "Why can't they just send me home and be done with it?" It felt like slow torture.

"I know. I thought they would, too, but sometimes you have to go and see the captain. Cynthia has noted that I'll be a witness if needed. I'm so sorry, Bianca."

Stunned, I stared out at the open sea, wishing the waves would pull me in and drag me away. Not only would I be fired from the ship, but I had to go up to the bridge in front of everyone and explain to the captain what happened.

I was sure people had done a lot worse. What about the olden days when the sailors used to poison each other? Maybe they were going to wait until Australia and feed me to the great whites or something.

I'd never been in real trouble before, and I was about to go on trial with the captain. Would I be handcuffed? Chained to the radiator like Jack in the Titanic?

"I hope I can go to see the captain as soon as possible so I can get my cases packed." I was welling up. "I need to let my family know that their failure of a daughter is coming home."

"Bianca, when you see the captain you should explain everything to him, and I mean EVERYTHING."

"What do you mean? I'd been drinking a bit too much vino and we were offered a threesome by a guest?" I asked sarcastically.

"No. You need to highlight the situation you've been in with your superiors. You know if you weren't so overworked and exhausted it might never have happened," Max suggested.

Max was right, that was certainly something to think about. I needed to let the captain know how hard I'd worked and what a difficult time I had experienced since I joined.

Captain Cooper seemed like a very firm but fair character. I wondered how he would take to my silly little staircase story which would be dragging him away from much more important matters. He was bound to be annoyed with me wasting his time. I went back to the office pondering my thoughts.

There was a letter on my desk when I got back, written in scrawny handwriting. It took me a while to decipher it to realise it was actually a complaint.

'Dear Newsletter Editor,

I read your daily paper every morning and night to enhance the experience of my cruise. I thoroughly enjoy your daily sunset and sunrise times on the front page as I like to watch the dawn come in and the dusk go out which I enjoy from my luxury suite with a balcony. Anyway, can you imagine my nephew's and my dismay this morning when we sat out on the balcony at 5.25am and the sun had already risen? You stated in your paper that the sunrise was at 5.26am when in fact we had just missed it by 1 minute 45 seconds. We are most disappointed and feel that our holiday has been ruined. We only booked this cruise for the spectacular daily sunrise and sunset. Can you please call me to advise what went wrong? Where do you get your calculations from? I will await your phone call.

Thank you, Cecil Smith - Suite 1201

Great. Just what I needed on a day like today.

After a few phone calls and an agreement of complimentary drinks and dinner on board, I'd finally made amends with the disgruntled guest.

Max popped his head around the office door. "Bianca, despite all this turmoil, we have still got a date with the kangaroos and koalas tomorrow, me, you, and Maddie."

"Am I still allowed to go out on tours?" I asked him.

"What's going to happen? Are you going to fall asleep in the wildlife park? Of course you're allowed." He dazzled his brilliant white teeth. "I hate to say this, but enjoy it while it lasts, my dear."

I was avoiding dinner time at the Officer's Mess for fear of all the questions, so I decided to carry on working and keep my head in the sand. Cynthia rang my office phone for me to come next door. I thought this was the moment of truth.

"Do sit down, Bianca. I have some news on your situation," Cynthia said. "The captain will see you up on the Bridge for a disciplinary hearing, as you have clearly broken the ship's code of conduct. However, that will be in a few days time, as he is so busy with the upcoming port of Australia and of course the Dinner Dance in Sydney."

"How long have I got to wait?" I struggled to speak. "I thought this would all be resolved by today?"

"Usually, yes, but we need the daily newsletter for our guests. Head office needs at least a couple of days to fly out your replacement."

I felt sick. I hadn't even had the meeting yet and they were already looking for someone to take over my job.

"I know this will be difficult for you, but I need you to stay focused. Keep doing your job and you will be present at the dinner as planned. I need you to welcome my guests."

I'd completely forgotten about the world cruise dinner. I was surprised that I could still go. I really did feel like Cinderella, but in reverse: I did not want to go to the ball. Not in this situation, no way.

How could I go there when I was in so much trouble? Especially when the captain would be there, too.

"I will continue with my duties as usual. Thank you." I left the office and sneaked off to my cabin for an early night. I didn't want to see anyone and I also needed to call home to let my family know what was going on.

"Bianca, I can't believe it. You have to tell the captain what's been going on. If he knows, he might understand your situation a bit more," my mother said.

"There's no point. I'm already gone. I'm just waiting for the meeting now," I told her.

"Don't be so silly. There's every point. It sounds like you've been given a terrible ride in your job, love. That isn't what you signed up for."

We said our goodbyes and I thought on my mum's words. I decided to take her advice. I would say my piece at the disciplinary to voice my side of the story at least.

It was my moral duty to let the captain know that the hours of the job needed to be looked at before the next unsuspecting bugger took over from me. I wouldn't have wished that stress on my worst enemy.

CHAPTER TWENTY-TWO
Kangaroos And Koalas

DATE:26 FEBRUARY 1998
PORT OF CALL: MELBOURNE, AUSTRALIA
AFTERNOON ARRIVAL: 12.00PM
ALL ABOARD: 9.00PM

I was absolutely horrified on my way to work. I took the usual stairs up to the office (those stairs) to find an outline of a body drawn out in chalk along the bottom steps. You know, like from a murder scene in a movie. If it wasn't aimed at me, I would have found that hysterical, but it just made me more upset.

"Oi, make sure you don't fall asleep." One of the waiters laughed as he passed me in the corridor, pushing a drinks trolley.

Obviously, the story was out and the gossip had started. Hundreds of crew members would be asking me what happened when I didn't want anyone to know. I ran back to my cabin to pick up a cloth and rubbed the stairs clean before anybody else could see. Not the best start to the day.

I dashed to Carl's office to tell him about the last night's events.

"I heard all about it, Bianca." Carl sighed heavily. "I've spoken to Cynthia about the way she was treating you and how upset you were, but in light of these circumstances I'm afraid it's fallen on deaf ears." He removed his glasses and rubbed his eyes.

"I wasn't unconscious. I was asleep and locked out," I muttered without much enthusiasm. I was tired of repeating the same thing over and over again.

"Look, it doesn't matter what I think, it matters what the captain thinks," Carl said.

"Are you going to mention that I'd been to visit you for help?" I questioned.

"Of course I am. That's what I'm here for. I'll fight in your corner, but it's classed as gross misconduct. I'm afraid you will be on the next plane home," he explained.

"I know I haven't got a cat in hell's chance of keeping my job, but I'm going to state my case to the captain just like I did to you," I replied defiantly. "I've nothing to lose now. I think the captain should know how some crew members are treated on board." I stood up to leave the room.

"There'll be ample opportunity for you to say that up there." Carl showed me to the door. "Ring me if you need anything, Bianca. Remember, I'm on your side and I cannot apologise enough for not getting to Cynthia sooner."

I thanked him and left.

I took a deep breath and made my way to work, pretending as though nothing had happened. I sat down at Max's desk.

"So shall we get this finished today?" I pointed to the dinner seating plan pinned to the wall behind him. "I want to keep busy."

"Yes. Let's box this off." Max pulled out his notebook. "This is never easy, despite me doing it the past few years. We have to sit the sailors with the navigators. The repeater guests like to sit between themselves. Your friends from the penguin club all need to be grouped together. It's like a massive jigsaw."

"Don't forget we need Giorgos near us, too. Who knows what mayhem he's going to cause," I reminded.

"I was thinking to put him on your table? You can keep an eye on him." Max laughed. "Let's go for a cup of tea."

"Ok, I'll come, but can we sit somewhere quiet?" I asked.

I was heckled twice en route to the mess about sleeping on the stairs. One guy who I'd never even seen before shouted down the corridor:

"When's the captain throwing you off?"

I hung my head in shame, wishing the ground would swallow me up.

"Ignore the lot of them. Just keep your head up and tell them to mind their own business," Max said firmly. "Anyway, we're gonna have a good afternoon at the koala park."

"Good, I can't wait, Max. Getting off the ship will clear my head a bit."

I looked up at the huge clock ticking away above the coffee machine. It was almost time to dock in Melbourne. You could feel the excitement in the crew as they were all buzzing around the canteen trying to get a glimpse of upcoming land through the port-holes. The prospect of being sent home so soon into this amazing adventure made me very sad.

After all those weeks of crossing the seas and the oceans, Lady Anne had finally hit Aussie soil. And it was a glorious sunny day with not a cloud in the sky.

I had to say goodbye to Skye and his band, it was time for them to leave.

"Bianca, you've been far out. Hopefully we'll see you at our concert in Sydney," said Skye as he gave me a high five. "Listen, can you give Giorgos my contact details? We had a wild night with him last night. That guy is off the hook." He winked at me.

I did not want to imagine what they got up to (!). He gave me the peace sign as he jumped into his waiting van.

Max, Maddie, and I were en route to see the koalas and kangaroos. We each had a tour bus of passengers whom we had to escort on and off the buses and around the park.

I had a Lady Anne paddle in my hand and all I had to remember was that I was tour guide eight on bus number twelve. I counted all my guests on the bus and introduced myself to the party.

"What's the weather like today?" one guest asked.

"We didn't hear you mention you were coming to see the kangaroos on your breakfast show," another quipped.

I was so preoccupied with worry I could barely even recall what I had just pre-recorded for the weather report. I laughed along politely, then quietly placed myself at the back of the bus, taking a seat next to a lady looking wistfully out of the window.

"Excuse me, do you mind if I join you?" I asked. "I'm Bianca, your tour guide for the afternoon."

"Of course, dear, do take a seat." The lady shuffled over to make space for me. "I'm Linda. Lovely to meet you. You probably get this all the time, but you're so lucky working on a ship like this. Your family must be very proud of you."

Maybe not so proud when I turned up on the doorstep back home with no job and no money. Still, I played along with Linda.

"So tell me, where do all you crew members live? On board? How do you get to work every day?"

I thought she was joking, but by the look on her face she wanted a serious answer.

"We all live below decks, actually." I answered as straight-faced as I could. "We live in the crew area downstairs, so it's just a short walk to wherever we work on the ship."

"That's such a good idea to have you all living and working on board. I did hear a rumour that you were flown out via helicopter at the end of your shifts and back again each morning." Linda laughed.

"How are you finding your cruise?" I asked.

"I love it. It's been a lifelong dream of mine to sail the world. I'm here for the full four months, you know, from Southampton to Southampton, and it has been wonderful so far." She lowered her voice. "It's my first holiday travelling alone. I had a bit of a messy divorce when my husband ran off with our landscape gardener."

"Oh, I'm sorry to hear that." I didn't quite know what to say.

"Please don't be, he did me a huge favour. I think I'm very lucky to have got out when I did. Now I can do what I like and experience places like this."

"That is such a great outlook to have. I hope I'm like you when I'm your age," I admitted out loud.

"Stick with me. I'm single and I'm ready to mingle." She winked.

We pulled up to the park and I counted off my guests from the bus into the entrance.

"Hi, mate! You can leave it here. I'm the park guide. Just meet me back at this gate in two hours." One of the park workers dressed head to toe in camouflage and a cork hat took my paddle out of my hands.

"I thought I was supposed to stay with the guests at all times?" I was confused.

"You've got a free arvo off, mate. You can go into the kangaroo pen or hold a koala." He shouted at the top of his voice: "Tour bus twelve follow me for an afternoon of Aussie adventures."

"Yooo hoooo." Max skipped over. "Isn't it great? We have our own free time? First stop obligatory koala photo." Max pointed to the really long queue.

"I'm not wasting time queueing in that to hold a smelly koala," Maddie tutted.

"Well, I am. I told my little brother I'd get him a photo so I don't care how long I wait." Max trotted off to the queue in a huff.

I didn't fancy waiting in that big line, either, not when it was the kangaroos I really wanted to see.

"Do you fancy the kangaroos then?" I suggested to Maddie.

"Yes, doesn't look like much of a wait, either." She hooked her arm into mine and off we went.

"There are five kangaroo pens here, so take your pick. We're not busy at the moment. Everyone's waiting to hold Kenny the koala," the attendant at the entrance told us.

"These kangaroos are running free, and you'll be in the middle of their habitat, so please stay calm. They won't harm you, they're just very curious and they'll love you if you feed them this."

I was handed a white paper bag of hamster-looking food.

We sat down at a wooden picnic bench in the middle, surrounded by lots of trees and bushes without a kangaroo in sight.

"Enjoy! Shout when you're done." The attendant locked the gate.

"Maybe we've scared them off?" Maddie whispered. "Let's just wait quietly."

We sat in silence waiting for a kangaroo to pounce. I pulled my bottle of water and the hamster food concoction out of my handbag and started shuffling the food around to make a rustling noise. No sooner had I done that than the nearby bushes started to move.

"They're coming!" I whispered to Maddie, looking at my half empty bottle of water on the park bench, feeling like we were in Jurassic Park.

"Really?" Maddie didn't move. She had her back to the bushes as the kangaroos began to jump out one by one.

"Sssssh! Don't move. Try to be quiet. They're coming right over."

There were five pretty big kangaroos hopping their way right over to our table. I was trying to stay calm.

"I hope they're not the boxing kind," Maddie hissed. "Is this safe?"

The animals were moving in closer as I continued rustling the food. They seemed to be very interested in the noise as they inched right up to us very slowly. Maddie was still frozen with her back to them when the biggest kangaroo leant right over her shoulder to get a closer look at the paper bag.

"I think they want feeding." Maddie whispered as the kangaroos were all circling our table. They were so close we could hear them breathing.

"I wonder if they'll let me feed them?" I put the dried food into the palm of my hand.

"They might have your hand off," Maddie warned.

I put my hand out and shut my eyes, waiting for one of them to act. I opened my eyes to find the smallest one nibbling from my hand. It was the sweetest thing I had ever seen.

"Get a picture!" I asked Maddie, who was scrambling in her bag for her camera.

"That one's stomach's moving." Maddie pointed to the bigger kangaroo, when out popped a little head from the pouch.

"Ah it's a little joey." The little baby had just woken up, with his big Bambi-like eyes staring at us. We fed them everything that we had and as soon as the bags were empty they hoped away, back into the bushes.

"Max is going to be so upset he missed this. I wonder where he is?"

"Let's go and find him." Maddie checked her watch.

We found Max at the park gates dressed very peculiarly and looking very pissed off. He was wearing a pair of camouflage shorts and the brightest yellow t-shirt which read 'Koalas are Kool'.

"Max are you feeling ok?" I was concerned as Max was usually impeccably dressed. "What happened to your chinos? Why are you dressed like a tourist?"

"I queued for an hour of my life to hold Kenny the koala." He starting raising his voice. "Why, out of everyone, did he decide to urinate on me? It wasn't just a little piddle either, I swear it must have been gallons and gallons of the worst smelling piss on the planet. I am mortified, violated, and I want my money back."

Maddie balked and I tried to stop myself from bursting into laughter.

"I was absolutely drenched in the worst stench ever. I had to beg to use the staff showers. I smelt so bad I had to throw my clothes away and obviously the only shop for miles is the koala gift shop."

He pointed to his outfit and kept shaking his head.

"Did you get a picture at least?" Maddie asked.

"Piss off, you," Max seethed.

"Let's do a quick bite to eat, girls. I'm starving," Max said as we piled out of the guest coaches. "I'm going to try and ignore my awful outfit."

We headed to a little restaurant on the beach in view of all the surfers catching the waves. It was perfect.

"Well, what a ride it's been so far." Maddie toasted. "To us three for making it all the way to Australia."

We had made it to the halfway point. Midway across the world on this crazy world cruise. It had been a roller coaster of emotion: the laughing, the crying, the excitement, the stress, the parties, the flirting, and we'd been through it all together.

"We've seen more of the world in these last few weeks than others see in a lifetime," Max said. "Just for the record, Bianca, I'm so proud of you. Whatever happens next, just look how far you have come. From the wide-eyed new girl terrified of doing the weather report to having your own guest fan club. Please don't just go back to dreary old England and stay there. Go wherever your wildest dreams take you! Life's too short."

I turned away, not wanting them to see that his words had brought a tear to my eye.

"Thanks, Max. It means a lot to me. Oh, you've got me all upset now," I wailed.

"Bianca, you're so funny." Maddie chuckled. "You'll do grand whatever you do. You've certainly cheered up my cruise since you arrived with your hundreds of cases on that gangway."

I really hoped that those two would be my friends for life, having shared this wonderfully weird experience.

I certainly felt a lot older and wiser than when I stepped on that ship in January. I had grown up a lot in myself and I'd even started to speak up for myself towards Cynthia.

Maybe my next career move could be giving out life advice when I got home, holding weekly meetings in the village hall and advising girls how to apply for jobs abroad.

Feeling very self righteous, we headed back to the ship arm in arm.

The office desk was piled high with to do files and notes which were definitely not there when I left. Then the phone rang.

"Bianca, next time you are going ashore please let me know in advance," Cynthia screeched. "It's Giorgos's Art Auction tomorrow, which is a terribly big event, yet you've been gallivanting all day."

"But I came in super early this morning and worked. I didn't leave with all these things on my desk." I protested.

"I know you didn't, because I put them there. Now, make sure they're done before you leave tonight." She hung up.

I took a deep breath and reminded myself how lucky I was to still be on board. It was two days to Sydney and the world cruise dinner. All I had to do was keep my head down and do my work.

CHAPTER TWENTY-THREE
Going Once, Going Twice...

DATE:27 FEBRUARY 1998

DAY AT SEA

ENROUTE TO: SYDNEY, AUSTRALIA

CRUISING THE TASMAN SEA

"You didn't organise any models for the live art demonstration?" Cynthia barked at Pete in the office. He looked at Cynthia blankly.

"Surely it is obvious you need to schedule models for a LIVE ART DEMONSTRATION?" she repeated.

"Giorgos didn't specify it was models. I thought it was going to be a bowl of fruit or something," Pete murmured.

"Well it's never been a bowl of fruit, you idiot! We need two human beings. Bianca, Max, go and get yourselves tarted up. It'll have to be you two," Cynthia ordered. "NOW!"

I'd spent all morning setting up the Art Auction in the ball-room, laying out the chairs like a real life auction and we even got the hammer from the prop department backstage. I thought all I had to do was help out moving the paintings. Now I was going to be centre stage and dressed in a bloody toga.

Cynthia was in a foul mood because Giorgos was a no-show for his interview on her breakfast show to plug his art auction, because he was too hungover.

"Who the bloody hell does he think he is?" She seethed as Max and I entered the ballroom. "First no interview, and now he's late for painting you two." She tapped her watch.

The crowds started to gather in the ballroom turned art auction. We had set up a perfectly cordoned off circle for myself and Max to pose in, and Giorgos to paint us.

"I'm never going to be able to keep a straight face." Max giggled in my ear.

"And you suppose I am?"

"Ladies and gentlemen. Welcome to the event of the cruise. Our Live Art Demonstration and Auction with the man himself. All the way from Athens, Greece, GIORGOS CARLOS!" Cynthia bellowed down the microphone as Giorgos strutted in to rapturous applause from the audience.

He was dressed all in white like some kind of angel, with his hair tied up in a perfect bun, looking like butter wouldn't melt.

"I just need a moment with my models as I give them my directive," Giorgos told the crowd.

He gave Max and I instructions: the scene was two cherubs whom had just been reunited again after an eternity apart.

How the hell was I going to keep a straight face?

There we were, channelling our inner cherubs, dressed in togas and wearing flower crowns, trying to be as serious as possible for the onlooking guests. Romeo and Juliet, eat your heart out.

We had to stifle our giggles as Giorgos very seriously narrated and painted us. It was like trying not to laugh at the headmaster in assembly at primary school, almost impossible. After what seemed like a lifetime, Giorgos finally announced his completion and took a bow.

"I shall reveal the finished item after my art auction. Ladies and gentlemen, please follow me." The throngs of people vacated the demonstration area to take their seats at the auction. Max and I gave each other a pat on the back as we were free to go back to our day jobs.

"Well, I never read 'love-struck cherub' in my job description," Max retorted. "Although you've probably got it next to fitness instructor."

We stood at the back of the ballroom, still in our costumes, and watched Cynthia take on the role of the auctioneer.

Giorgos's paintings were flying out and at thousands of pounds, too. The crowd gasped in amazement as the top painting sold to a penthouse guest for ninety thousand pounds.

"Bloody hell, you can buy a flat for that," I whispered in Max's ear.

The art auction came to a close as Cynthia thanked the crowd and Giorgos gave a thank you speech.

"That was a job well done." Cynthia clapped as she and Giorgos walked towards us. "Thank you to our models."

"Thank you, Miss Cynthia." Giorgos winked. "Would you like to meet me for a drink tonight?"

"I can't, I'm doing a jazz set in the Chart Room." Cynthia blushed and made her excuses to leave.

"Let's celebrate!" Giorgos took a swig straight from a champagne bottle. "We've made a small fortune today."

"I can't, Giorgos. I've to go back to my real job now," I explained, unwrapping the flower crown from my hair.

"Then I insist you accompany me to afternoon tea in the restaurant. I have a very important business proposition for you, Miss Bianca."

I was very intrigued as to what this business proposition could be. Did he want me to be his full-time live art model, flying all over the world with him? I could get used to that.

"What about me?" Max asked, looking rather disappointed he wasn't included in the conversation.

"Sorry, Max, this is strictly between myself and Bianca." Giorgos flounced off to get another glass of champagne.

I waited eagerly outside afternoon tea for Giorgos to arrive. I had special permission to attend the tea from Cynthia, as the Art Auction had been such a success. Giorgos sauntered up to me all dressed in black again, with his hair flowing loose like the rock star he was.

"So glad you could make it." He kissed me on both cheeks.

"Thank you for inviting me." I noticed a silver hip flask sticking out his trouser pocket, probably to pour in his afternoon tea cup.

A waiter showed us to our table for two towards the back of the restaurant, right next to the big windows.

"I guess you're waiting for me to reveal my idea to you?" Giorgos asked as the white-gloved waiter poured our tea from a silver pot. "I've been watching how you work since I came on board, and I must say I'm very impressed with your work ethic."

"Thank you, that's very kind. We work incredibly hard on this ship."

"As you know, I'm based out of New York now with my new gallery coming up." He looked around to see if anyone was looking and quickly topped up his tea up with whatever was in his silver hip flask.

"My PA is based there and she's just resigned. She got a new job in Miami."

I sat looking wide-eyed, very keen to hear the next part of his sentence.

"So my question is: would you be interested in filling that position?" He looked very pleased with himself.

"I don't really know much about art," I blurted out.

"You can learn, Bianca. The PA does my admin work. I'm the artist. Why does the PA need to know about art? You just need to know my schedule, and make sure I show up to my stuff."

I couldn't believe what I was hearing. I had just had about the worst week of my life, and there I was sitting with a world famous painter being offered a job in NEW YORK! Me! I was delighted.

"Giorgos, I'm so flattered and honoured you think I could fill such a position."

"So what do you say?" he asked.

"Don't I need a visa or a green card or something?"

"Yes, that's the catch. We'd have to get married," Giorgos replied. My face dropped.

"I'm joking, Bianca." He laughed. "I'll check with my lawyers to see how we would get you the right paperwork."

I didn't want to get my hopes up too much until I knew it was definite, but oh my word what an amazing opportunity.

I said my thank yous and skipped out of afternoon tea on a high. I would keep quiet about it until something materialised.

I went straight back to my cabin after work. I wanted an early night for the madness of the next few days. Lisa was on the bed, painting her nails and pampering herself.

"I'm so excited, mate," she told me as I walked through the door. "I'm meeting all my Sydney friends tomorrow. I really want you to come."

"I'd love to Lisa, but I can't." I had too much to do.

"You're going to have a great time, though. I wish I was meeting old friends tomorrow, you lucky thing."

I changed into my pyjamas and dived into bed, dreaming about my next career as a Manhattan PA. Life did have its swings and roundabouts.

The pager buzzing woke me up in the middle of the night. I jumped out of bed in the darkness, fumbling for the thing. I rang the number that was flashing, expecting it to be my boss.

"We're sorry to wake you at this time of the morning," a very official voice said down the phone. "This is Terry from security. We need you to come to the CCTV room and help us with the identification of a guest."

"What's wrong? Has somebody hurt themselves?" I asked, picturing me pointing out bodies in the morgue below decks.

"Quite the opposite, but we do need your help in identifying certain faces. Please get ready and come up as soon as possible."

As I was still half asleep, I got lost three times until I eventually found the security office. I had to get one of the night watchmen to show me where it was. It was very well hidden.

"Thank you for getting here so quickly," Terry said, locking the door behind me.

"No problem. What can I help you with?"

"There is a situation in the Jacuzzi on deck eight aft. It's been going on for a while." Terry looked at his watch. "I'm about to go and intervene, but I need to be certain who I am dealing with here. I'll say no more. See for yourself." He led me over to the dozens of cctv camera screens covering every part of the ship. I quickly scanned for the dreaded staircase and breathed a sigh of relief that it wasn't there.

"It's this camera." Terry sat down and zoomed in on the jacuzzi cam. I sat down next to him to get a closer look.

OH MY GOD! It was Giorgos in the Jacuzzi, wearing an officer's hat and smoking a cigar whilst guzzling from a bottle of champagne, but that wasn't all. He was in there with two other ladies.

One was clearly one of the bar waitresses, and the other guest I immediately recognised. The lovely lady I was chatting to from the kangaroo tour, Linda. She wasn't kidding when she said she was ready to mingle!

"Obviously, that is one of our crew members blatantly breaking the ship's standing orders." Terry shook his head. "I wanted you to confirm if this was the celebrity speaker we have on board?"

I reluctantly nodded my head. I didn't want to get anybody into trouble, but the evidence was there to see. I cringed as Giorgos emerged from the Jacuzzi, butt naked, to get more champagne, and it didn't look like the other two ladies were wearing much, either.

"Thank you for confirming for me. I shall wake up Cynthia now as she'll have to come with me when I approach this very seedy situation. You may go now. Thank you, I just wanted to be sure." Terry showed me to the door.

"What about the guest? Will she get in trouble?"

"Of course not. She's a paying customer."

I was relieved to learn Linda would not be involved.

"But that crew member will be on the next flight home."

I walked back to my cabin feeling quite dismayed. After being so excited at the prospect of a new job working for Giorgos, now that didn't seem like such a wise career move.

CHAPTER TWENTY-FOUR

From Southampton To Sydney

DATE: 28 FEBRUARY 1998

IN THE PORT OF SYDNEY, AUSTRALIA

ARRIVAL: 6.00AM

ALL ABOARD: OVERNIGHT STAY (5.00PM THE FOLLOWING
AFTERNOON)

The big day had finally arrived. The 5.00am sail into Sydney
Harbour. Excitement spread like wildfire. Most of the ship's crew
were up early on the open decks to watch the sail in. We were
docking right next to Sydney Harbour Bridge and just across the
water from the Opera House.

Cameras were flashing and whirring away as the morning
sunlight bounced off the water, lighting up the bay around us.

"We have successfully sailed the world from Southampton to
Sydney!" Max and Maddie cheered with our morning cups of tea.

I, Bianca Drake, who'd never left England before, had just sailed
half way around the globe and all on my own. I'd crossed the world's
oceans, making it all the way to Sydney, Australia. I'd never forget
that moment for as long as I live.

Pete was hovering around the office door, waiting for me to arrive so he could fill me in on the night before's antics as I got to work.

"I saved you a job. Giorgos is on a final warning from none other than the captain." Pete looked rather flustered. "I have it in writing. One more incident like this, and he and his paintings will be sent packing."

My heart sank as the reminder of my imminent hearing with the captain was getting closer.

"I was going to go and speak to him just now, Pete."

"Don't worry, it's done. Cynthia thought it'd be better coming from someone in a little more authority." He jokingly straightened his tie, making himself seem more important.

"The other lady guest inside the hot tub has asked that we keep this matter confidential." He shook his head. "Honestly, you couldn't make this shit up."

"Will Giorgos still be allowed to the dinner?" I asked.

"That's another thing, I can't attend the dinner as I have to hold the fort here whilst Cynthia is off. Can you please keep a very watchful eye on him for me?"

"Of course I will, Pete. He's seated on my table, even."

"Now go and enjoy Sydney, you lucky bugger. Some of us have to work all day."

I finished my work and left a note on Cynthia's desk to let her know I'd be gone for a few hours.

Max, Maddie, and I met up at the cruise pier to begin our day of Sydney sightseeing. First up we visited the Opera House to take the obligatory tourist photos against the backdrop, then we went over to the bridge to take in the views. Some of the braver crew were doing the bridge walk with full harnesses and everything, walking all the way to the top. I shuddered as it gave me flashbacks of my bungee jumping date (with he who shall not be named) in Auckland. I would rather chew on glass than walk up to the top. Heights were never my idea of fun.

We hailed a taxi and made our way to Bondi. The cab was a yellow one just like the Manhattan cabs. We were giggling in the taxi as Max recalled the New York leopard incident to Maddie, yet again.

"Did you hear about the bar staff girl, Francine, who was in the hot tub with Giorgos?" Maddie asked as she silently drew a her finger across her throat.

"She's gone already?" I squeaked, picturing me being next down the gangway.

"They had her on camera. There was no denying it." Maddie laughed. "I don't remember reading it was allowed to have an orgy in a hot tub with guests is the ship's code of conduct."

The taxi pulled up at Bondi Beach. It was lot smaller than I had imagined, but just as beautiful with the white sands and the clear blue sea. We took more tourist photos at the beach sign.

"Bianca! Bianca!" Coming right towards me was Lisa and her Sydney friends, complete with beers in hand and a sound system blasting out techno music.

"Here she is. This is my roomie, Bianca, all the way from Great Britain." Lisa introduced me to all her friends. I couldn't really make out what Lisa and her friends were saying, as they were all shouting over each other. One of the boys started swinging me round the beach, then lifted me up and dropped me on the sand. I was covered in sand and stone cold sober.

"So do you wanna meet later?" Lisa was slurring her words and not quite focusing her eyes on me. "I'll give you a call, yeah? I ain't coming back till tomorrow morning, mate." She staggered off towards the water with her friends in tow.

"Well, weren't they a hoot?" Max noted. "Did you see the one with the cap on? He was hot."

"He definitely didn't bat for your team," Maddie piped up. "He was giving me the eye, not you. He looked a bit like that gorgeous Daniel from Honolulu." Maddie went all gooey eyed as she reminisced over our Hawaiian beach party.

"Did you ever hear from him again?" I asked.

She shook her head. "Nope. Pointless anyway. I say that if we don't meet our soul mates within the next five years, we make a pact to emigrate here together and find ourselves our very own Australian dreamboats."

Max and I very enthusiastically agreed. I could definitely see myself living there.

"I'm so nervous about tonight. I feel like we're going to my wedding or the Oscars or something major. My nerves are shredded," Max exclaimed.

"It's going to be a brilliant event," I reassured Max. "And also, my last night on board. Let's make it a night to remember."

We rushed back to the office to finish the last minute preparations. I found a card and a gift wrapped up on my desk.

I wondered who it could be from. I opened the card to find a huge thank you message inside:

Dearest Banca,

I want to thank you so much for looking after me whilst on board your ship. You really did make my time extra special. I very much look forward to working with you again next year. Here is a little something which I think might help you on your journey through love and life - I hope it helps you find your Prince Charming.
Best Wishes, Dr. Christine x

Bless Dr. Christine. She never did get my name right. I sort of guessed what the gift was going to be, and sure enough as I tore the gift paper off, it was one of her bestselling hardbacks.

'Top (Sex) Tips for Single Ladies'

Complete with a personalised message and phone number to keep in touch. I flicked over the top tips, all very similar to her lecture with plenty of banana references. What a sweet gesture from a wonderful lady.

It was pamper time for the big event. I had everything ready on my cabin floor in order of precision: face pack, rollers, cosmetics, nail polish, eyelashes. Stick on eyelashes were never my strong point. One was stuck to my eyebrow whilst the other one ended up glued to my cheek. I was just about to give up after many profanities when, hey presto, they fit perfectly into place. I sprayed a bit of perfume and ruffled my bouncy hair loose.

Then it was time for the dress. My gorgeous fairy princess/ Greek goddess/Cinderella dress. It was one-shouldered and the perfect shade of pale blue. I put my high heels on first, then stepped into the dress which was in a perfect circle on the floor, then lifted the dress up around me.

I managed to get it over one shoulder, then all I had to do was zip it up at the back, but I couldn't reach it. I tried using the hook of a coat hanger to no avail. Eventually, I popped my head out of my door and scanned the corridor for anyone passing by to help me squeeze into it.

Thankfully, I found a housekeeper in the corridor and begged her to come and help. After five minutes of pushing, pulling and breathing in, I didn't think it was going to happen. Then, as if by magic, it did.

"You look like a pretty princess, Miss Bianca," she said as she finally got the zip up.

I was so relieved. I had my dream dress on and it fit perfectly, give or take a few ribs. I decided not to eat much at the dinner and minimise my breathing pattern: pain is beauty and all that.

I quickly rushed out my cabin to go and meet Cynthia. The world cruise annual dinner was upon us and I could not be late.

CHAPTER TWENTY-FIVE
Sydney Soiree

DATE: 28 FEBRUARY 1998
IN THE PORT OF SYDNEY, AUSTRALIA
ARRIVAL: 6.00AM
ALL ABOARD: OVERNIGHT STAY (5.00PM THE FOLLOWING AFTERNOON)

Cynthia couldn't fit her gown into the car. She was wearing a huge lemon crinoline gown, flowery from every angle, and covered in daffodils. I had to practically shove her in.

"Thank you, Bianca. You look very presentable."

Wow. A compliment from Cynthia; even if she did force it out.

"I need to run over my welcome address." Cynthia looked a little nervous practising her speech out loud on the journey there. She sounded as insincere and patronising as ever with the usual shouting down my ear. After the long and awkward drive, we pulled up outside the town hall.

The town hall was an impressive building. A red carpet led up the steps to the huge cast iron double doors. The building had stood there since 1889. Just like our ship, the town hall was enriched with history. Max had chosen this venue for our dinner himself, once Cynthia agreed, obviously.

At the entrance, a youth choir sang beautifully as people entered.

"Please offer these to all the guests at the door." Cynthia shoved a box of pretty peach flower corsages into my arms.

My first job of the evening, and I could stand and listen to the choir sing. Three hundred corsages and 'Good evenings' later, I was relieved by Maddie.

"It's my turn now, girl. By the way you look stunning," she said, admiring my blue Cinderella gown.

"Thank you. You look like a film star, Mad." She looked wonderful in her long black and silver fishtail gown.

"Ok, it's almost show time. Can you go and check that everybody is almost seated?" Cynthia asked.

Inside, the dinner hall looked fantastic. Seas of beautifully decorated candlelit tables were adorned with flower arrangements and set against a backdrop of the biggest church organ I'd ever seen. The pipes reached from the floor to the top of the very high ceiling. It was breathtaking.

"You're the hostess of table 18. Be sure to cater to our guests' every need. Keep the conversation going and keep their wine glasses topped up. About the wine, just stick to one or two. We don't want you falling asleep now, do we?" She smirked.

I ignored her comment and walked up to my designated table to announce myself. I had to constantly remind myself to breathe with the bodice of my dress digging in my rib cage.

"Good evening, gentlemen. Welcome to the world cruise dinner!"

My party stood up to welcome me. Sure enough, as Max and I had perfectly planned, I was seated with Giorgios, John, and Jeremy (my fans of Bianca guests).

"We're so happy we get to spend our last night of the cruise with our favourite weather girl!" John exclaimed.

"Me too! I'm delighted. Who are we missing?" I pointed to the empty seat.

"Giorgios politely asked us if our friend would swap seats for his friend," Jeremy informed me.

"Who are we expecting?" I asked Giorgios, feeling slightly annoyed that he had changed the carefully planned seating arrangement I had spent so much time on.

"I hope you don't mind, Bianca, but I took the liberty of inviting my new lady." Giorgios smiled.

"Who?" I was baffled.

"Allow me to introduce you to a wonderful woman I actually met here on board." He stood up and beckoned over his companion to join us. "Gents, Bianca, this is my lovely lady, Linda."

Images of the Jacuzzi CCTV footage flashed in my mind as I grimaced a smile.

"Hi, Darling." Linda kissed me on both cheeks. "Don't mind if I join you, do you?"

As soon as Linda sat at the table, she and Giorgios began to fawn over each other like love-struck teenagers.

"So guys! How was your cruise? I can't believe it's your last night!" I struck up conversation with Jeremy and John.

"And what a place to spend it. Sydney town hall is a fabulous setting for a fabulous occasion!" Jeremy toasted.

"Isn't she old enough to be his grandmother?" John whispered to me.

"Just keep smiling and pretend it's not happening." Jeremy nudged John in his side.

The waiters began to serve a fancy, delicious dinner, yet the food did not deter Linda and Giorgios from whispering sweet nothings into each other's ears.

"She will be my muse. She is my Lady Anne Sophia Loren." Giorgio stroked Linda's hair as she giggled. I didn't know where to look. It was very, very awkward.

"About that job offer, Bianca." Giorgio turned to within my earshot. "Linda and I are planning to trek around Tibet, so I am going to have to postpone my offer until further notice."

"I see." I tried not to look disappointed. I was going home the next day and my only possible job offer was disappearing in front of my eyes. I couldn't quite believe it.

Thankfully, the stage lit up and the band started to play. Just as I thought things couldn't get any more uncomfortable, I spied Cynthia marching over to my table, squeezing her dress between the tables and chairs to get to me.

"Can I have a word?" she barked. "In private?"

My heart sank as I wondered what on earth I could have possibly done wrong again. I excused myself and followed her down a long corridor that led to a dimly lit courtyard full of smoking party-goers.

"Wait here. I'll be back in just a moment," Cynthia said, lifting her gown above her heels and disappearing out of sight. I sat down on a wooden bench, taking care not to rip my own dress or breathe too deeply as I was waiting for her return. She showed up a few minutes later with two shot glasses and a packet of cigarettes. I didn't know she smoked or drank. I glanced around the yard to see who she was bringing the drinks for. She sat herself down next to me and passed me a glass.

"Down the hatch, Bianca." She held her glass up for a cheers. I didn't respond as I didn't know if this was some kind of set up.

"Come on then?" she repeated.

I clinked glasses with her and downed the shot. It was straight vodka and it almost blew my head off.

"Would you like a fag?" She offered me a cigarette from the packet she was clutching.

I didn't usually smoke, but after this little episode, I guessed I was going to need one. I obligingly lit up.

"I'm going to be sad to see you go, you know." She inhaled a drag of her smoke. "I know you're shocked. I admit I'm not the easiest to work with, but I want you to know, I have enjoyed having you on board."

After all these months, Cynthia La Plante was actually being civil with me. I was flabbergasted.

"I push my staff to the limits, because I want my team to be the best they can be. I sometimes unintentionally get carried away and push too far. Perhaps this is what has happened in your case, and I am truly sorry for that." She looked down into her empty shot glass. "I've worked so hard to get to where I am today. I think overcoming struggles in life makes you appreciate a lot more who you are and what you become."

"So you don't hate me?" I blurted out. The vodka had given me a bit of Dutch courage.

"Of course I don't, Bianca." She looked me straight in the eye. "I know you won't believe this, but I see a little bit of me in you, when I was your age. I'm sorry it's come to this." She put her cigarette out and stood up. "Come on, let's enjoy the rest of the night."

We walked back to the dining hall.

Dinner was served, then it was time to dance again. Max and Maddie were a pair of naturals, gliding across the dance floor like Fred and Ginger.

None of my table wanted to dance, which was just as well, as I had no coordination for ballroom dancing, accompanied by two left feet.

I stuck to Cynthia's advice and just had one glass of wine to toast with the guests.

"Bianca, can I have this next dance?" a voice asked.

I turned around and to my disbelief it was Captain Cooper. Asking me to dance! The room seemed to zoom in on me by 150% and I began to feel slightly dizzy. The following two scenarios sprung into my mind:

a./ I would probably stand all over his toes.

b./ I am on trial with him in the morning and the outcome depended on how well I could cha cha cha.

Oh shit! I wanted the floor to swallow me up, but I put a brave face on, joined the dance floor, and attempted to waltz. Well, Captain Cooper waltzed and I just stamped all over his toes.

I kept apologising as he kept trying to lead me. It was so surreal, here was the guy who my job and future depended on, twirling me around the dance floor. All I could think about was about the hearing the next day, in between getting the moves completely wrong and looking like an arse. I felt like Nelly the elephant dressed up as the sugar plum fairy.

Maddie and Max weren't helping either, bursting into fits of laughter when the captain had his back to them. Finally, after the four longest minutes of my life, I was free, the song was over.

"Thank you, Miss Drake. Can I suggest you polish up on your dance steps? You almost scuffed my shoes." The captain laughed.

I gave my apologies and sat down to watch the rest of the dancing.

"Right. Come on, back to the ship. Ball gowns off, hot pants on. We're going clubbing Sydney style," Maddie exclaimed, pulling me and Max together. I shook my head. I needed to have a clear head for tomorrow.

"Bianca, you are coming. How often do you get to party in Sydney?" Maddie looked horrified.

"You don't have to get wasted. This is your last night and our last night together." Max backed her up.

I suppose you have noticed by now that I'm no good with peer pressure, thus I usually cave immediately. But for once I acted like a responsible adult.

"No, I can't guys! Please put yourself in my shoes. I have to face the music in less than seven hours."

This time I put my foot down as reality smacked me right across the face with an invisible spade. I could feel a huge black cloud coming back over my head. I was going home tomorrow, going home to normality, to my dreary little town with no job or money.

Tomorrow was dawning upon me, and I had to get my shit together.

CHAPTER TWENTY-SIX
Judgement Day

DATE: 29 FEBRUARY 1998
IN THE PORT OF SYDNEY, AUSTRALIA
ALL ABOARD: 5.00PM

I didn't sleep much, terrified of the day's outcome. With a heavy heart, I got ready for the big hearing. I placed all my suitcases outside my cabin, ready to be picked up. Lisa rolled in with an ice pack on her head, still in the clothes from the night before.

"Shit got messy last night, mate." Lisa sat on the bed nursing her forehead. "I met up with all my Sydney mates and I got plastered, like totally plastered."

"I know, I met you at Bondi Beach," I reminded her.

"No, I didn't?" She looked bewildered. "I didn't go to a beach. I went on a bar crawl, mate."

I didn't prod her any further and passed her a cold bottle of water from our little fridge. I felt bad for her. She looked a lot worse than I felt.

"Anyway, I passed out in the taxi on the way home to the ship, like completely out cold. The taxi driver didn't know where I was going and he couldn't find any ID on me, so he dropped me off still asleep at the local cop station."

"What happened?"

"Well, he still couldn't wake me up and neither could the cops, so I woke up this morning in a prison cell." I waited for her to laugh, but she was being deadly serious. "I spent the night in a Sydney jail cell, like I was in prison, mate."

"Oh my word, you poor thing. Are you alright?" I sat on the bed next to Lisa and put my arm round her.

"Pretty scary stuff. I hate myself. I'm never drinking again."

"What did the police say?" I asked.

"They let me off with a drunk and disorderly fine. Thank god they didn't find my ship ID on me or they would have contacted the ship and I would have been a goner." She gulped from the bottle of water.

"Thank heavens you got away with it," I reassured her as my thoughts flashed to me confessing of my sins to Captain Cooper in just a few minutes time. I felt like I was on death row and today was the morning of the dreaded gas chamber. What the hell had I done?

I wanted to kick myself. This was supposed to be a job of a lifetime and I'd messed it all up in a matter of weeks. I wiped a tear from my eye.

Max met me at my cabin for moral support, and of course he was going to give his account of the night in question.

"I have to tell you, Max, Cynthia bought me a drink last night and said she actually liked me?" I confessed. "I'm very bemused by it all."

"Did she really? That's a first." Max gasped. "She might feel guilty for what's happened with you. She needs to stop being so hard on her staff."

"It was a relief to see a little bit of a soft side of her," I admitted. "We shotted straight vodka and smoked. How random." I stopped dead in my tracks took a deep breath and fixed my hair. "Ok, Max. I'm ready to face the music!"

"Good. You're so bloody brave, Bianca. Just so you know, I have my speech all up here." Max pointed to his head.

As we got to Cynthia's office, I took a long deep breath before I knocked on the door.

"Come in." I entered the room looking as traumatised as I felt.

"Bianca, don't look so worried, the worst is over. I watched you attempting to waltz with the captain last night."

Was this an attempt from Cynthia to make light of the situation? I wasn't sure whether I was meant to laugh or she was ridiculing me, but I really wasn't in the mood.

"Last night was a rip-roaring success, so thank you both, especially Max. Without you that event wouldn't have been possible." She straightened herself up in her chair. "Do you know what to expect today? I believe neither of you have been to a captain's hearing before."

"We're going to trial and Bianca is the accused?" Max muttered under his breath.

"The hearing is very formal. You must stand with your hands behind your back. Only speak when you are spoken to, except when it is your time to give your side of events. There will be witnesses taking notes for the captain, and you will both receive a copy of the investigation."

I felt like I was in an episode of Murder She Wrote. I wondered if they had a typewriter up on the bridge.

"Shall we?" Cynthia signalled to make our way up to the bridge and the captain's quarters.

This was it. Judgement Day. We took the elevator all the way to the top of the ship. My mouth was completely dry and my tongue was glued to the roof of my mouth. Max handed me a small bottle of water he had in his bag.

How was I supposed to give the talk of my life when I had no saliva in my mouth? In complete silence, we walked through the NO ACCESS doors and then we got to the captain's office.

"Wait here. I'll see if the captain is ready for you." Cynthia went into the office.

"Bianca, don't get so worked up. What's done is done. Just make sure you get your story across." Max squeezed my hand.

Cynthia beckoned us to the office. This was it, the moment of truth.

The captain sat at his desk, holding a huge file which was obviously my report. His secretary sat to the left of him and Carl was on the right.

I stood facing the captain with Cynthia to my left and Max to my right. We all stood with our backs straight and hands behind us, very regimental like. I glanced out the huge window looking over Sydney Harbour. This was so surreal. I felt like I was in a living nightmare.

"So let me begin." The captain ruffled his papers.

"We're here to talk about the night of Miss Drake being found on staircase 13, deck 1. Can you recall that evening?" he asked.

"Yes, sir," I replied.

He then began to read the case file out loud. The report from the Hit Squad, the medical team, and of course, my boss. I was cringing and closing my eyes as the report made it sound so much more dramatic than it actually was. It made me feel even worse.

"Do you agree that is what occurred on that evening?" the captain asked.

I nodded in silence.

"You'll all be given the opportunity to give your version of events. What I need to determine from this meeting is whether or not this was gross misconduct. Failure to comply with the ship's code of conduct usually means instant dismissal. In this instance, due to the busy schedule of the world cruise, I have had to postpone this meeting. My apologies for the delay." Captain Cooper was stony-faced.

My heart was pounding.

"First of all, let's begin with Cynthia, your head of department, who was disturbed at an ungodly hour of the night." He nodded to Cynthia. She reiterated to the captain the statement he read out earlier.

It was then Max's turn to recall the night's events, detailing how I came to be locked out of my cabin.

I began to feel the dry mouth again, but this time I was also sweating profusely, becoming more and more nervous as it was coming up to my turn to speak.

All I could hear was 'Bianca not eating,' 'lost weight,' 'working too many hours every day'. I couldn't focus on what Max was saying anymore. I felt dizzy and the room was spinning.

Nerves had truly taken over me and my knees were knocking. There was no way I was going to be able to hold my speech, shaking, with my hands and knees rattling.

"Are you ok, Bianca?" the captain asked me.

"Yes, sir. I just wish it was over with. I feel as though I've killed somebody," I wailed.

"Have some water, and when you're ready, we're ready for your side of the story." The captain stared at me.

I cleared my throat. I had to get my side across loud and clear.

"That evening, I had worked a very long day, and finished work around 8.00pm, so I went to the crew bar to watch the band play, then I went to meet our VIP guest in the piano bar," I began.

"After that I went back to my cabin with Max, when I realised that I had forgotten to send an important message for work. I left my cabin and went up to the office to send the email." My nerves had calmed slightly and my voice began to strengthen.

"I went back down to my cabin, but I was locked out, so I sat on the staircase which was just opposite of my cabin to wait. I was tired, so unfortunately I dozed off. Next thing I knew, I was in a wheelchair being told I had fallen down the stairs and knocked myself unconscious. I tried to tell the medical staff I had not fallen, but they wouldn't listen. Obviously they had procedures to follow, which I fully understand. The rest of the statements you read out to me were also true, that is exactly what happened, and I apologise for it all profusely."

I paused to let the secretary catch up writing her notes. I think everybody thought I was finished, but I had something else to say.

"Captain, I would like to say my piece, if I may?"

"Go ahead, Bianca."

"I'm incredibly sorry for getting myself into this situation, but I must stress the circumstances of the situation I was in." My knee-shaking had minimized, but my voice had begun to quiver again. God help if I ever was on a real trial. I wouldn't last five minutes in a magistrates.

"From the moment I joined this ship, I've been working over and above the hours I was supposed to. I've been given mammoth tasks without any support from anyone. I've been so busy, I haven't been able to get off the ship on several occasions to see some of the wonderful places we have been visiting."

The captain listened intently as Cynthia stood with a very false grin on her face.

"Some days I have worked up to fourteen hours just trying to catch up. I haven't been eating properly, either, as I have been too busy to take rest breaks. I know I've messed up and I must be sent home, but I want to make all of this known to you, Captain Cooper. I don't want the next secretary who fills my position to be under the amount of stress and pressure I have endured."

I stopped for a minute to drink some more water. I was more composed now, as I knew I was getting to the end of my statement.

"I asked for help from various people, including HR, and have been in tears on several occasions over my workload. Unfortunately, due to the lack of rest and not eating properly, I'm afraid I was in the wrong place at the wrong time and fell asleep on the staircase. Had I been getting proper rest and breaks, I'm sure I wouldn't be in this situation. Now, here I am before you, facing dismissal."

I was becoming more emotional as the words came out, and it became more and more apparent that the whole thing just wasn't fair. I worked my arse off in that job.

"I've had to wait a week for this hearing to take place. In that week, I have been humiliated every time I am in the crew areas, with staff asking 'Are you still here?' and 'When are you getting fired then?' It's been horrendous and I wouldn't wish it on anyone." I couldn't hold my emotions back anymore, and the tears started streaming down my face and I began to cry in front of everybody. The last thing I wanted.

"Is this true, Cynthia? Have you been allowing this girl to work that amount of hours?" the captain questioned.

"It is true that she has a great workload to deal with, as the job role in question requires a lot of hours," Cynthia replied.

"Have you done anything to ease that workload?" the captain raised his eyebrows.

"I offered to help or get her help," Cynthia answered.

"Did you follow this up as well as ensuring she was getting proper rest and eating properly?" the captain asked.

"Of course," she replied.

Of course she didn't. If she had I would never have been in such a sorry situation. Max shot me a reassuring glance across the room.

"So you got her help to ease her workload?" the captain prodded Cynthia further.

"Not exactly." Cynthia had her head down this time, speaking very quietly.

"Ok, Bianca, can you and your witness leave the room? We will call you back once our investigation concludes," the captain ordered as he reshuffled his papers.

Outside in the corridor, I grabbed onto Max as I thought I was going to pass out. Max sat me down and fetched me some more water.

"You did great. At least you spoke the truth." Max hugged me tightly.

I was so relieved to get my side of the story finally out in the open.

"I just want it all over with." I sobbed, wiping my tears from my face. "This whole episode has totally drained me."

It was time to go back into the office and return to our military like positions. I felt slightly calmer. At least the worst was over.

"We have reviewed your case, Bianca, and are ready to continue. We will now deliver the outcome," the captain said.

"Having reviewed the situation, there is no getting away from the fact that you were asleep on the staircase. This is gross misconduct, which 9 out of 10 times results in instant dismissal, to which my hands are tied," he continued.

I nodded in agreement.

"Given the circumstances that you were in, I agree it was a difficult situation, and no one should feel this way on board as part of the ship's crew of Lady Anne."

I just wanted him to hurry up so I could go and get my bags.

"You asked for help, and you were not given the correct support to help you overcome your on-board work schedule. Correct?"

"Correct, sir."

"Therefore, I've decided that your case constitutes the 1 out of 10 that does not result in dismissal." He snapped the file closed.

Why did everyone look so happy all of a sudden? Captain Cooper's words were not registering in my brain properly. Max was looking at me eagerly for some kind of reaction, but I was not understanding.

"I mean to say, Bianca, considering this unique case, I have decided not to dismiss you. You are an invaluable member of our team. I am, however, placing you on a final written warning, so you must be on your best behaviour going forward. Case dismissed."

What just happened? I was stunned. I was staying? I wasn't fired?

It took a minute or two for me to respond.

"Thank you so much, Captain. I don't believe it. I have my cases packed and everything." I was crying again, but this time it was tears of relief and happiness. I was staying!

"It's also the responsibility of your head of department to have your workload reduced and give you the correct support you need."

Cynthia nodded in agreement.

"If the job gets too much for you again, come and see me directly," the captain said sternly. "Now go. I don't want to ever have to see you in this capacity again, Miss Drake."

I floated to the elevator in a daze. Was I really staying or had I dreamt what had just happened?

"You're the first person I've ever seen to be excused by the captain in all my years at sea. Consider yourself very, very lucky." Cynthia patted me on the shoulder. "For what it's worth, Bianca, I'm very happy you are staying. Congratulations." She looked quite emotional as she left Max and I alone in the elevator.

"Did that just happen?" I was bewildered.

"Bianca, you've been saved!!" Max jumped up and down as we hugged. "That was one of the most dramatic things I've ever seen."

I was absolutely over the moon. Never would I look at a set of stairs the same again!

CHAPTER TWENTY-SEVEN
Riots And Reunions

DATE: 5 MARCH 1998
PORT OF CALL: PORT DOUGLAS, AUSTRALIA (THE GREAT BARRIER REEF)
ARRIVAL: 6.30AM
ALL ABOARD: 6.00PM

Five days had passed and I woke up glad to be alive and kicking on the good ship Lady Anne. I was up at 6.30am and packing my kit for the gym. Lisa rolled in still with the same clothes from the night before, looking rather tipsy as I was leaving the cabin.

"You're bloody lucky, mate. Struth, you should have walked the plank." Lisa hugged me. I couldn't breathe much. All I could smell was the cigarette ash she had managed to store in her hair.

"I know, you remind me every day, Lisa. You need to sort yourself out, love. We're docking in an hour you need to be at work."

After all the drama of the past week, I had decided it was time to turn over a new leaf and focus on exercising and getting fit rather than being the social butterfly I was before. I'd been given a second chance and intended to make the most of the opportunity. Besides, I could do with losing a few pounds with my newly acquired pot belly.

"We have a problem, Bianca," Cynthia barked down the phone. "We can't get into Port Douglas today due to high winds. I need you to come and make an emergency newsletter."

Since I had embarked Lady Anne, we'd never missed a port. Cynthia had warned me it was a lot of work, because a sea day's worth of activities had to be scheduled last minute, and I had to mass produce a revised newsletter confirming the new schedule. Within the hour.

I dropped my gym idea and ran up to the office.

"You have missed a space there." Cynthia was pointing to my computer screen over my shoulder, literally breathing down my neck.

I had to note down Cynthia's revised schedule word for word, then she was scrutinising my words. It was very nerve wracking having her hovering over me whilst I was typing.

"You don't spell Sigourney like that." She slapped herself in the forehead as I was typing in the afternoon movie. The woman was so highly strung I could've played her in an orchestra.

"You know, I'm not sure how the guests are going to take this. The great Barrier Reef is one of the highlights of the voyage." She shook her head and tutted.

She seemed to be opening up to me for some empathy or compassion, but I was so busy sweating on adding the 'u' to Sigourney that I didn't respond. A spelling mistake to me was like a noose around my neck. Her phone rang and she left the office.

"Good morning, ladies and gentlemen. I regret to inform you that due to extreme weather conditions, we will not be arriving to Port Douglas this morning. On behalf of the captain, myself, and the ship's company, we sincerely apologise. In thirty minutes, a revised sea day newsletter will be distributed to your cabins with today's activities. Thank you for your cooperation." Cynthia's voice blared through the PA system.

Half an hour. Jesus Christ, I needed to pull my finger out. I was only half way through and we still had to get the thing printed.

"Let's get this show on the road." Cynthia barged back in and positioned herself over my shoulder again.

"That should say 2.00pm not 2.00am. For goodness sake, Bianca, from now on I am going to call you the cut and paste queen." She breathed heavily down my ear.

I smiled and nodded and kept reminding myself how grateful I was to still be on board and with my job intact. With ten minutes to spare, we were done and dusted, and the paper had gone down to the print shop to be duplicated.

"There's a really bad vibe around the ship today," Maddie commented as we walked to lunch. "Word of warning. It's probably a good day to keep out of the guest areas. They'll pounce on anyone in uniform. By the way, did Max get hold of you? He needs to speak to you."

"He called me earlier at my desk, but I couldn't speak as I had Cynthia with me," I replied.

"I only booked this trip to see my son in Port Douglas," I heard a guest complaining to the receptionists as I walked by. I felt so sorry for the girls on desk with the huge queue of disgruntled passengers.

"Aren't you the weather girl?" One little old lady grabbed me firmly by the arm. "Who do I speak to with regards to arranging compensation for missing today?" she demanded.

"I'm afraid we have missed today's port due to weather restrictions which are out of our control." I sounded like I knew what I was talking about, but still the little old lady didn't look too happy.

"I want a word with your boss. The Great Barrier Reef is a once in a lifetime. I've paid bloody good money for this trip."

Another man shouted: "Cynthia is the one who made the announcement."

I made my excuses and escaped from the reception desk as fast as I could, sensing tension coming from all directions.

When I got to the officer's mess, a stressed-looking Cynthia was in the line front of me. When I informed her that the guests were demanding to speak to her, she looked dismayed and went to sit with the captain at his table.

I was back in the office trying to work, but finding it increasingly difficult to concentrate with the dull rocking. The ship was starting to move as the winds picked up. The phones kept ringing and all I could hear was poor Pete having to explain about the missed port. After the tenth phone call he looked like he was about to have a meltdown.

"I've been on the phone all day apologising and it's still only midday." Pete put his head in his hands.

"You should see the reception desk. It's still packed." Max closed the office door quickly behind him and held himself against it. "I hope they don't find this office or we will be lynched."

"Send them to Cynthia's office, then," I suggested.

"Bianca, I need to speak to you in private when you're not busy," Max reminded me.

"Sure, Max, later on."

"Guys, we need to have an impromptu meeting." Cynthia arrived, closing the door tightly behind her, looking quite pale.

"The passengers are in uproar. They seem to be rallying up some kind of protest. They are utterly furious they have missed today." Cynthia took off her glasses and rubbed the lines in her forehead. I almost felt sorry for her, almost.

"I haven't seen a reaction like this since we missed Port Stanley off Argentina in 1988. This is very rare." She shook her head.

"Well, what do we do? How do we keep everybody calm?" Pete asked.

"I'm not sure we can. If there is a mutiny it is usually beyond our control," she replied.

A mutiny? Were we on a cruise ship or the 'Jolly Rodger'?

I was having visions of Cynthia using me as the gopher and sending me out to apologise to everyone.

"They're gathering in the ballroom as we speak. There are a couple of instigators, and it's regular sailors we have with us." She pointed to me. "Bianca, you must come with me to the ballroom to investigate."

I knew it. I knew I would be dragged into this. We crept backstage of the ballroom so we could peer through the stage curtains to see what was going on.

"WEEEEE SHALL!, WE SHALL NOT BE MOVED!
WEEEEE SHALL!, WE SHALL NOT BE MOVED!"

I peeked through a small gap in the curtain to see a good few hundred passengers shouting at the top of their voices and clapping. In the middle of the crowd were two gentlemen who seemed to be riling everybody up.

"We've paid thousands for this trip. Just because there's a tiny bit of wind, we've been cancelled. We want answers!" One guy was stamping his feet and punching the air.

"Nobody has even bothered to explain to us in person exactly what's going on. Where's the captain?" another guy asked.

"WE WANT THE CAPTAIN! WE WANT THE CAPTAIN!" The crowd began to shout in unison.

This was going from bad to worse. These passengers had been on board for too long. After all, it had been three straight months for them on a ship not doing much except playing draughts and overindulging on afternoon tea. Cabin fever had hit fever pitch.

"WE WANT THE CAPTAIN! WE WANT THE CAPTAIN!" The chants were getting louder and more aggressive.

"I can't let this go on. I have to intervene." Cynthia began scrambling for a backstage microphone.

"WE WANT THE CAPTAIN! WE WANT THE CAPTAIN!"

"Order, order, ladies and gentlemen!"

I rolled back the curtains as Cynthia stood centre stage. The whole room went silent as Cynthia went into great detail about wind speeds and north swells to try and appease the angry crowd.

"We don't want to hear it from you. We want the captain!" one of the elderly guys piped up.

"WE WANT THE CAPTAIN! WE WANT THE CAPTAIN!" Everyone started again.

Cynthia was still trying to explain over the microphone, but the crowd drowned her out. When they started booing and hissing her, she fled the stage looking rather flustered.

"Please call up to the bridge for back up, Bianca."

I called up and got through to Officer James.

"I'm on my way." He seemed happy to intervene. "Nothing I can't handle Miss Weather Girl."

I thought it was a brilliant idea that James was coming to the rescue. He would probably start talking about himself and how brilliant he was and then bore all the protestors to sleep.

"I'm going to lie down in a dark room. Tell Officer James he can issue everyone with a $50.00 on board drinks voucher as compensation for their loss." Cynthia left, leaving me to relay the information.

I passed the information onto James and quickly left to film the weather show for the next day.

I was so excited to do another weather report. I mean, I could've been on a plane back to old, boring, cold, wet England. I was very lucky by all accounts.

"You'll be pleased to know, ladies and gentlemen, that we're now sailing into calmer weather and smooth seas as we head on to our next port of call: Kota Kinabalu, Malaysia, otherwise known as Borneo, 'home of the Orangutangs'. Max and I intend to go walking with the orangutangs in the wild. I'll let you know how we get on. That's all from me. Have a good day."

I was still getting carried away with these port day plans, but I didn't care, I was so happy to be there. Anyway, we did want to walk with them, we just had to find out how and where.

"I'm so sorry, Max. I've been rushed off my feet all day. It's been non-stop." I apologised as I was filing my papers away for the next day. "What a day, hey?"

"Good old Officer James defused the situation with his good looks and charm." Max scoffed. "I've been trying to tell you something ALL day! Guess who is coming back next port?" He asked, smirking at me.

"Go on, who? Sergiy, your Russian dancer guy, is he back?" I wasn't really paying attention as I'd far too much work to do.

"No, guess again." Max smiled.

"The French passenger who wants you to move to Paris?"

"No, yuk!" He shook his head. "He was far too old."

"The flute player who proposed to you at the midnight buffet?" I was getting fed up. I just wanted him to tell me.

"Bianca, please sit down and listen!" I closed the filing cabinet and sat down, wondering which one of his ship lovers had turned up out of the blue.

"Bianca, it's your officer! He's on his way back! I've good word from a very reliable source that he's finished with his girlfriend at home. Like for real. He doesn't want her anymore. I wonder why that could be?" Max clapped his hands together in delight. "His father is ok now, so he's coming back to the ship in five sea days time to be exact. When we dock in Malaysia!" Max waited eagerly for my response. "Go on - say something? Anything?"

To say I was shocked was an understatement. I certainly wasn't expecting to see him again. What a pleasant surprise.

Maybe ship life wasn't so bad after all...